Charley slid into his seat at the table and folded his hands. "Can I say grace?"

"You bet. Give it your best shot, buddy," Will said.

Catherine listened in amazement as the child began to pray.

"Dear God, thanks for fish, especially salmon the way Uncle Will cooks it, and for cabbage even though it's gross. And thank you for Jesus and my mom and my uncle and for Miss Catherine who's come to help us fix up Hope House. And take care of Gram. You're lucky you've got her now. Amen."

Catherine didn't even realize there were tears streaming down her face until Will touched a napkin to one cheek.

"He affects me that way, too, sometimes," Will said so softly that Charley, who was busy eating, didn't hear.

Everything Charley and Will did seemed to touch Catherine to her core. She looked down at the napkin in her lap. She didn't want Will to see her face. She was a hairbreadth away from falling for these two charmers, and what a complication that would be.

Books by Judy Baer

Love Inspired

Be My Neat-Heart
Mirror, Mirror
Sleeping Beauty
The Cinderella List
Mending Her Heart

Steeple Hill Single Title

The Whitney Chronicles
Million Dollar Dilemma
Norah's Ark

JUDY BAER

Angel Award-winning author and two-time RITA®
Award finalist Judy Baer has written more than
seventy books in the past twenty years. A native of
North Dakota and graduate of Concordia College
in Minnesota, she currently lives near Minneapolis.
In addition to writing, Judy works as a personal life
coach and writing coach. Judy speaks in churches,
libraries, women's groups and at writers' conferences
across the country. She enjoys time with her husband,
two daughters, three stepchildren and the growing
number of spouses, pets and babies they bring home.
Judy, who once raised buffalo, now owns horses. She
recently completed her master's degree and accepted
a position as adjunct faculty at St. Mary's University,
Minneapolis, Minnesota. Readers are invited to visit
her website at www.judykbaer.com.

Mending Her Heart
Judy Baer

Steeple
Hill®

Published by Steeple Hill Books™

STEEPLE HILL BOOKS

Steeple
Hill®

ISBN-13: 978-0-373-81534-0

MENDING HER HEART

Copyright © 2011 by Judy Duenow

www.SteepleHill.com

Printed in U.S.A.

Weeping may tarry for the night,
but joy comes in the morning.
—*Psalm* 30:5

For my mom. I love you.

Chapter One

Goodbye, Gram. I love you.

Catherine Stanhope turned away from the grave site, her heart aching, unable to watch the ornate silver casket being lowered into the ground. Now the last living Stanhope, she felt truly alone.

As she turned away, consumed with grief and loneliness, she stumbled on a patch of rough ground and pitched forward. She would have fallen flat on her face but for a pair of strong hands that quickly circled her waist.

"Are you okay?" Will Tanner studied her with dark, compassionate eyes.

"Fine, considering the circumstances." Her voice was faint and monotone.

She stared down at her feet as if they belonged to someone else. She'd worn ridiculously high heels to the funeral even though she knew full well that she'd have to make her way across the cemetery to the elaborate Stanhope family headstone that towered over the rest of the graveyard's modest rows of tombstones. She wasn't thinking ahead. In fact, she wasn't thinking at all. The sudden death of her grandmother Abigail had come as such a shock that she was still reeling.

Instead of letting the man go, Catherine gripped his arm even tighter to balance herself, kicked off her shoes, picked them up and sighed. "Sorry. Thank you." She smiled imperceptibly. "Gram never liked high heels. She always told me I'd break an ankle in these things some day. I certainly don't want it to be today." Her grandmother had always been practical and no-nonsense.

"That sounds just like Abigail," he agreed pleasantly.

Catherine looked at him curiously, studying the fine planes of his face and thick, expressive brows. Since she'd arrived in Pleasant, Minnesota, she'd been inundated with the funeral details that left her sad and exhausted. She hadn't made the connection between Mr. Will Tanner and her grandmother until meeting him in the mourners' gathering room before the service. "How long did you say you've been working for my grandmother?"

"Nearly six months."

An unexpected wave of envy swept over her. Tanner, a virtual stranger, had spent more time with her grandmother than she had in recent weeks.

She was responsible, she knew. Gram had called her a dozen times asking when she was going to take time away from work to come home for a visit.

She'd always given the same answer. "I can't get away, Gram. I have trial dates set and a desk full of cases to address. Why don't you come to Minneapolis? We'll go out for dinner every night. You'll be able to browse all the bookstores and libraries you love. It would be good for you to get away, too, you know…."

Gram had come, of course, but it wasn't the same. Nothing matched a visit with Abigail Stanhope at Stanhope House—or Hope House, as the locals called it. Being surrounded by family art, heirlooms and history or sitting on the back porch sipping tea with the woman who'd raised her, were opportunities Catherine had taken for granted until it was too late. The regret tasted bitter in her mouth. And it only deepened the grief that already overwhelmed her. All she could do was steel herself against the pain.

"Shall we go to Hope House, dear?" Emma Lane, her grandmother's best friend, was waiting for them by the last few of the parked cars. "Are you ready?"

Catherine had chosen to stay with Emma the past two nights rather than spend them alone at Hope House.

"People are coming by. The church ladies are serving lunch at the house. Your aunt Ellen and uncle Max went ahead to welcome the guests."

Catherine pressed her thumb and forefinger together over the bridge of her nose to ward off the headache that was lurking behind her eyes. "Yes… but I'd like a few minutes to myself first."

Emma, with whom Catherine had ridden from the church, looked concerned. "Of course. I'm sure they'll realize they need to plug in the coffeemaker…."

"You can go back to Hope House and do what needs to be done, Emma. I'll drive her back to the house," Tanner offered. "That will give Catherine as much time as she needs."

Catherine shot him a grateful glance. The past few hours had been a maelstrom of emotion. Add to that the traumatic and stressful days she'd had at work preceding her grandmother's passing and Catherine felt emotionally battered and utterly weary. Right now ten minutes alone was like hitting the mother lode.

After Emma had gone, Catherine turned to Will. "Thank you for giving me a few minutes to collect myself. I really haven't had time to process any of this." It was as if she'd been walking in a dream… no, a nightmare…since Emma called. She flashed back to three days earlier.

"Catherine? This is Emma Lane." Catherine

had grown up eating gingersnaps out of Emma's fat ceramic cookie jar, a rotund brown chicken with a red comb and orange beak, and playing in the gazebo in the Lanes' backyard.

Emma sounded as if she'd been crying. "I hate to disturb you so early in the morning, dear, but your grandmother has suffered a stroke. She called me last night to say she wasn't feeling well and was going to bed early. I can't say why, but I woke up at 5 a.m. with Abigail on my mind. I tried to go back to sleep, but I couldn't shake the urge to get up and go to her place to check on her."

Catherine felt her stomach plunge as if she were barreling downward on an out-of-control roller-coaster ride.

"It was as if God Himself prodded me to get up, so I did. I have a key to the house because we occasionally check on each other's plants and furnaces." Emma's voice quavered. "I found Abigail unconscious on the floor between the bed and the bathroom."

"No…" The wail Catherine heard was her own.

Emma paused to regain her composure. "I called 9-1-1 and went with her to the hospital. She's gone, Catherine. She never woke up."

Catherine stumbled again, the pain in her heart threatening to bring her to her knees.

Tanner took her arm. Catherine stiffened but didn't withdraw as he steered her toward a nearby

Mending Her Heart

garden bench, one of several scattered throughout the cemetery. A small bronze plaque on the concrete base said, "Donated by the Stanhope Family, 1996. *Do not let your hearts be troubled. Trust in God: trust also in Me. In My Father's house are many rooms; if it were not so I would have told you. I am going there to prepare a place for you. And if I go and prepare a place for you, I will come back and take you to be with Me that you may also be where I am. John 14:1-3.*"

She sank onto it gratefully. "I'm sorry I'm holding you up. It's very kind of you to stay with me."

"I'm happy to do it. Anything for Abigail and her family."

As she studied him from her perch on the iron frame, he rested one hip on the arm of the bench, crossed his arms over his chest and smiled slightly. "I can see you are full of questions about me."

She *was* full of questions, but she didn't realize it was quite so visible. Gram had told her she'd found a caretaker and groundskeeper for Hope House. That had been a great relief to Catherine. Hope House was far too big a project for an elderly woman alone. But Gram hadn't said that the hired man looked like an Adonis—tall, strong, athletic, dark-haired and staggeringly handsome. That, no doubt, she'd wanted Catherine to see for herself. Gram enjoyed surprises and he was certainly one.

A rabbit hopped in front of the bench and paused

to stare at them with a curious eye. Neither of them moved until the rabbit grew bored with them and bounded off.

It was soothing to sit here beneath the canopy of trees and be with someone who demanded nothing of her.

Ironic, she thought, that even now, despite the loss of her beloved gram, she felt more like herself than she had back in Minneapolis in the vortex of complex legal issues that had been her life. Here, at least, she knew that Gram was now where she'd longed to be for years, ever since Catherine's grandfather Charles had died. Gram looked forward to heaven the way some people look forward to monetary reward or success. Heaven, for Gram, was the priceless inheritance and ultimate success.

A finger of sadness moved through her gut as her thoughts hopscotched over the events of the past few weeks. Now she would never get the chance to tell Gram that she hadn't lost her mind by quitting her lucrative and prestigious job at the law firm. She longed to tell her grandmother why she'd so suddenly left her job, put her home on the market and decided to come home to Pleasant to regroup and consider her options. There was the offer to teach at the law school, of course, which was practically a done deal. She had only to sign on the dotted line. Then a former client now in state government had dangled a political-appointment carrot in front of her, and a friend in Maine had called seeking her expertise. She'd been counting on Gram to affirm her next move, whatever it might be.

Abigail Stanhope had been her wisest champion and most loyal confidant since the day Catherine had arrived as an orphaned little girl on Abigail's doorstep. The idea of life without her grandmother was impossible to comprehend.

Of course, Catherine thought bitterly, this season in her life seemed to be one of relinquishing things—job, home, and now…

"Catherine?"

She started at the sound of Will Tanner's concerned voice and brushed a hand across her eyes to push her long blond hair away from her face. "Sorry. I drifted off, didn't I? Shall we head back to your car?"

"Have you had enough time?" His voice was so gentle that it made her want to cry. His chiseled features were inked with concern.

"I don't think there *is* enough time," she said with a weak smile.

He took her elbow and guided her toward his vehicle. Unconsciously she moved closer to him, unexpectedly hungry for human warmth and tenderness.

"I'll bet I know where Abigail went first when she got to heaven." His voice softened into something that sounded both sad and amused.

"I don't understand."

"She told me that the first thing she wanted to do when she got to heaven was to go to the information booth and ask all the questions she'd been saving up. Why God made wood ticks, for example."

Catherine felt a bubble of laughter well in her chest. "That sounds just like Gram. Did the two of you talk about those things a lot?"

He paused before answering, as if carefully considering his choice of words. "Your grandmother introduced me to God. Most of our conversations were either about faith or the house. Those were her favorite topics."

"I see." She was taken aback by the admission. Gram and Mr. Tanner had shared a very personal and meaningful experience, then. This employee-employer relationship ran much deeper than she'd first assumed.

It shouldn't have surprised her, really, knowing Gram. She ran everything in her life through the filter of God. What would He think? Want? Encourage? That's how she lived her life. Gram never cared what other people thought. If God was good with something, that was all she wanted.

"Abigail also told me that you recently quit your job," he added casually.

"She did?" Catherine didn't know quite what to make of the fact that Gram had told him about her life.

He smiled again, wistful this time. "We spent a lot of time drinking coffee at her kitchen table. I would remind her we needed to be working, but she would insist that civilized people took regular breaks." He chuckled a little. "She made me *very* civilized."

That, Catherine knew, was exactly how Gram functioned. *She* should have been the one spending these last days with Gram, not some stranger. It was her own fault. She was the one who'd put off coming home.

"If only I'd come home a few days earlier! I was almost ready to leave the Cities when Emma called. I was able to pull on clothes, throw already-packed suitcases into my car and be on the road in less than thirty minutes."

"So you'd been planning to come to Pleasant anyway?"

It was what she'd always done whenever she needed to recharge. She'd already stored her personal belongings in a storage space and arranged for a Realtor to begin showing her house once she vacated it. There was nothing to stop her from leaving the city for as long as she wanted.

"Yes." She'd assumed there would be a time when she and Gram could curl up in massive wingback chairs, sip peppermint tea and discuss the twists and turns her life had taken, as they had done so many times over the years. Then Gram would pray for her.

That was what Catherine found herself most hungry for right now. She closed her eyes and sighed.

Will studied Catherine Stanhope intently. He hadn't expected her to be so beautiful.

Abigail had warned him that her granddaughter was easy on the eyes. He just hadn't known how easy. Will immediately chastised himself for being so crass at a time like this, but he knew if Abigail were here she would have been tickled by his surprise. "See? I told you!" she would have chortled gleefully.

But she was gone and her granddaughter felt frail and fragile against his side as they walked slowly to his pickup truck. Her long honey-gold hair tumbled over his arm in a glistening wave and her profile, when he glanced at her, seemed carved from porcelain, smooth and pale. Long black lashes fanned over her cheeks and tears hung from them like dew.

He felt as if he'd been punched in the belly with a battering ram at the idea of losing Abigail. What flood of emotions must this woman be feeling?

Although he knew better, Will had somehow assumed that Abigail would be around forever; that her indomitable spirit would allow her to survive no matter what. They'd had dinner together just two nights before her death. While Will made ribs on the grill, Abigail had whipped up a batch of her special slaw. They'd finished with coffee and huge slices of coconut cake and watched the sun go down together. And now she was gone. He couldn't get his head around it, at least not yet.

He'd been proud to say, "I work for Abigail Stanhope." Present tense, he thought. That wasn't right anymore. He'd *worked* for Abigail. Past tense.

If only there were something he could do for Abigail's granddaughter to ease her pain, Will thought helplessly. The only thing he knew to do was to show her that Abigail's wishes for the house were being carried out even after her death. Perhaps that would be a comfort to her, but now was not the time.

"This is your vehicle?" Catherine asked, forcing him to study the beat-up club-cab truck he used for construction jobs. It never occurred to him to back his sporty Camaro out of the garage anymore. Pleasant was a pickup truck kind of place and he liked it that way.

"Sorry." He saw her distressed expression and, feeling a flicker of annoyance, opened the door and began to brush nails, paint-chip samples and bits of molding off the front seat. "I didn't realize I'd be having a guest on the way home." The only other person he'd ever apologized to for the state of his truck was his sister-in-law, Sheila. "I am a groundskeeper and carpenter, you know."

"I'm sorry. That sounded snippy. I've been around

too many people who think of cars as status sym-
bols. Gram would have scolded me roundly for
that."

She looked embarrassed. Will appreciated that.
Snobbish women like his sister-in-law turned him
off. He didn't want Catherine to be one of those
because he was drawn to her, even under these difficult circumstances.

He helped her into the cab, pulled out the seat
belt for her and then circled to the driver's side of
the truck. For some reason he felt as if his life had
just become terribly complicated.

Chapter Two

Catherine didn't speak as they drove through town but reclined against the seat back, vacantly watching buildings go by. Stanley's Meat Market, Wilders' drugstore with its original soda fountain and the Stop-In gas station. The doors were open on several of the rooms at the Flatley motel, being aired out for the next guests.

They pulled up to the front gate of the Stanhope mansion, an impressive three-story structure with wide porches, ornate gingerbread trim and white lace curtains blowing in the windows. There were cars everywhere, parked down both sides of the street and in neighboring driveways. More cars, it seemed to Will, than there were in the entire town of Pleasant. Abigail had been a well-loved woman.

The geraniums in the huge metal vases that flanked the stairway and the front door were a

vibrant red. The variegated hostas Abigail loved so
much marched, lush and beautiful, around the foundation of the house. Will had stripped and repainted
every baluster with care and was pleased with the
results. The porch railing looked brand-new. Abigail
had loved it…. Will fought back the emotion swelling in his chest. At least she'd had the opportunity
to enjoy it before she died.

As he helped Catherine out of the car, she looked
at him again, with those sad gray-green eyes. When
she grabbed his forearm to steady herself, Will felt
an unexpected frisson of energy make its way up
his arm. Was he feeling electricity between them?

You're just plain stupid if that's what you think.
He was merely a convenient pillar to lean on. He
could have been made of wood or plaster for all
she cared. He felt closer to her than she to him only
because Abigail had talked so much about her.

"Thank you," she said softly. She tipped her head
to look at him and he saw gratitude in her eyes.

Well, maybe she cared a little.

"I'm very sorry about your grandmother. She was
one of a kind."

Catherine smiled faintly. "She certainly was. I
still can't believe it's true." She looked at the massive
home before her, its gleaming windows and glossy
gray porch floor sparkling back at her. "Maybe once
I've been inside I'll realize she's gone."

I wouldn't count on it, he thought grimly as he

followed her into the house. This place was as alive with memories of Abigail as a house could possibly be.

Still carrying her shoes, Catherine stared up at the mansion that was her childhood home. This was where she belonged right now, she realized, as she was swept up in an overpowering sense of rightness, of home. This was the repository for her family's history, this quaint step-back-in-time place. It was particularly true of her great-grandfather, Obadiah Elias Stanhope.

Obadiah had come from Illinois in the late 1800s and opened a small bank on Main Street. A savvy man who wasn't afraid of either risk or criticism, Obadiah had, during the Great Depression, amassed a number of failing banks and invested prudently. Thus the Stanhope banking fortune was born and the Stanhope name embedded in the very fabric of the town. He'd built a mansion for his beloved wife and son and, eventually, daughter-in-law, Abigail. Now she, Obadiah's great-granddaughter, was the only remaining Stanhope. What might Obadiah have expected of her? He was a man of grand ideas and splendid schemes. A weighty blanket of duty and obligation settled around her shoulders like a thick wool cape, unwieldy, confining and fraught with responsibility—the very things she'd tried to leave behind in her law practice.

She could see people milling around inside the

house, holding coffee cups and plates of food. Mr. and Mrs. Flatley, owners of Pleasant's only motel, were there, awkwardly balancing plates of food on their knees. Even the gentleman from Stop-In station was there, though Catherine knew he was relatively new to town. Others were on the wide expanse of porch, including Stanley Wilder and his wife, who ran the drugstore. In fact, everyone who'd ever lived in Pleasant seemed to be present. Aunt Ellen, her mother's sister, was pouring coffee from a silver server and her uncle Max was handing around a tray of dainty sandwiches that the church ladies had provided. It was a party Abigail would have enjoyed.

"Ms. Stanhope?" A deep male voice rumbled near her ear.

A large, gray-haired man came into her line of vision. "I'm Dr. Benjamin Randall, Abigail's physician. She was a wonderful woman, your grandmother, good to the hospital and very gracious to me. This is a great loss for everyone who knew her. My condolences."

As the big man's intent blue eyes bored into her, Catherine was suddenly overcome with a shortness of breath. She opened her mouth to respond, but when she took one step forward, it was as if she were being moved by puppet strings. Confusions overtook her. Then someone cut all the strings and Catherine slipped to the ground in a dead faint.

She awoke to the anxious faces of Will, Emma, Uncle Max, Aunt Ellen and several of her grandmother's friends peering down at her as she lay on the lumpy horsehair couch Abigail had insisted was Obadiah's favorite. There was worried muttering in the background.

"Sorry, I…I…" she began. Then a plastic dump truck landed on her chest. Following it was the face of a small boy with shaggy brown hair, deep brown eyes, round pink cheeks and a hopeful expression.

"My dump truck always made Grandma Abby feel better," he said with sublime innocence. "You can play with it if you want." Then he smiled at her, the sweet, trusting smile that children usually save for the people they love most.

The wall around her heart softened and she reached her hand out to the boy. Before she could speak, a familiar but frowning dark figure swooped down on the child and picked him up.

"This isn't the time or place, little buddy," Will Tanner said to the child. "It's very nice of you to offer to share your dump truck, but I don't think Ms. Stanhope is in the mood right now. Let's get you a soda."

"But Grandma Abby said if everyone would put their problems in my truck and send it to the dump, they'd all be happier," the young voice piped. "Don't you want that lady to be happy?" His words grew farther away as he was spirited into the kitchen. A hint of laughter spread through the room.

Emma, looking relieved that Catherine had stirred, helped her to her feet. "That's Will Tanner's nephew, Charley. He's only eight and hasn't quite grasped the fact that Abigail is gone. He was only trying to help."

And he had, Catherine thought. He'd interjected some lightness into the dark moment. She was grateful for something tangible to do away with the disconnected feelings she was experiencing. The child was right, too. She'd love to send her current toxic troubles to some faraway place. He'd also reminded her that she did have control over how she responded to what was before her. She'd have to thank Charley later—and find out exactly why he was calling *her* grandmother "Grandma."

She was not the only one in this room who was grieving. Besides, Abigail would have expected her to recognize that, Catherine reminded herself. Just because she was steeping in a brew of vulnerability and grief, she still had responsibilities. She had people to greet. What she couldn't do for herself, she would do for her grandmother. That included being a gracious hostess for those who'd come to pay their respects.

She rose from the couch with a weak smile. She was accustomed to hiding her emotions from a jury. She could do it here, too. "No harm done. I haven't eaten much today. I was just a little faint, that's all." She waved a hand toward the milling guests. "Please, keep visiting. Don't worry about me. I want this to be a celebration of my grandmother's life."

Reluctantly at first, and then with more gusto, the guests began to talk among themselves, telling stories about Abigail and even erupting into laughter at the memories. Catherine made her way to the vast dining-room table where a buffet was set up and picked up a sandwich so she'd have something in her stomach. Then she moved from group to group accepting the sympathetic comments and gestures of affection the people of Pleasant had to offer.

"Catherine!" Mrs. Margolis, her third-grade teacher, grabbed her by the hand and embraced her in a hug that nearly suffocated her. The dear woman still wore White Shoulders perfume after all these years. Eddie Henke, the milkman, looked distraught. Abigail had befriended him many times and he wanted to tell Catherine about each of them.

One by one, people approached her to tell Catherine the ways that her grandmother had blessed them—making donations to the park fund, paying doctor bills, buying braces for a needy child. But as she moved toward a group of people from Gram's church, she was brought up sharply. "Catherine, we have to talk."

The tone of Aunt Ellen's voice brought her to a halt. Automatically, Catherine steeled herself. She loved her aunt even though they rarely saw eye to eye. This was the one conversation Catherine had hoped to avoid today, but there was no way to stop the inevitable.

"So," Ellen said, "I hear you left your job in Minneapolis." Her face puckered as she said it, as if the words were distasteful. Ellen was pencil thin and dressed to the nines. Her hair, cut in an asymmetrical bob, looked like a piece of architecture. She was wide-eyed and unlined thanks to the nips and tucks she used to fend off old age. Unfortunately Ellen had also removed much of the personality from her own features. She was still beautiful, though, as had been Catherine's mother, Emily.

Her mother's sister was a force of nature, Catherine had learned long ago, accustomed to getting her own way and not a terribly gracious loser when foiled. The only person she'd ever seen stand up to Ellen and win was Abigail. It was back then that Catherine first understood the power of a mother lion fighting for her cub.

"That's right. My plans are fluid for the time being. There's no hurry for me to go back." She chose not to mention the job offers she'd had. She didn't want Ellen's input right now, and because Catherine was leaning toward teaching, she would have the rest of the summer at Hope House. "I can stay in Pleasant as long as I need to." Catherine could tell her aunt didn't think that was fortunate at all.

"What about your home?"

"I put my condo on the market this week. No use doing things halfway." She'd already emailed her housekeeper to store the few things that were left. Then she'd texted her Realtor to tell her the house would be ready to show next week. When she was ready to move on, there would be nothing tying her down.

"It sounds like you're burning bridges. You've certainly made sure you can't go back. What are you thinking, Catherine? Yours was a very prestigious job."

"I suppose, if that sort of thing impresses you." And that was just the sort of thing that did impress her aunt. Conrad, Connor & Cassidy—the Three C's as the staff called them—had a highly regarded reputation. "To me it was just my work—family law."

"But you held other people's lives in your hands!" Ellen pointed out. "You had the ability to change their futures. That's very important."

Too important, sometimes, Catherine thought. She didn't want to be responsible for the world. She didn't want to be accountable for anything right now. She'd never been completely comfortable with courtroom drama. Nor did she want to carry the burdens of other people's heartbreak on her shoulders.

One of her last cases had proved to be the proverbial straw that broke the camel's back. A custody case, it had involved all the drama, intrigue and heartache of an afternoon soap opera—deception, trickery, deceit and revenge. Sadly, a small child had stood at the center of the swirling controversy. That was what had bothered Catherine most.

"It also wears a person out emotionally," Catherine said to Ellen. "It's difficult to stay aloof from the issues and the people involved without becoming calloused."

She didn't want to be a cynic who kept people at a distance, avoided personal relationships and concentrated only on the work. She hadn't liked the person she was becoming.

Impulsively Catherine threw her arm around her aunt and gave her an affectionate squeeze. Even that didn't stop Ellen from expressing her opinion. "It sounds like a disastrous decision to me," she said. "Throwing away a lucrative career…and for what?"

Some things just never change, Ellen's quest for income and status being one. She and Uncle Max had been kind to want to adopt her, Catherine thought, but it never would have worked.

"I like to think of it as an opportunity," Catherine said frankly, "a chance to reinvent myself. There's a profession out there that doesn't drain my energy and steal my spirit." *Like teaching, perhaps.*

Emma and Will approached at that moment, saving her from any more of her aunt's comments. Ellen walked away, shaking her head.

"Don't mind your aunt," Emma said gently, obviously having overheard the conversation. "Her intentions are good. She has different values, that's all. You've always been a sweet girl with a very tender heart. Your grandmother wondered how you could be in such a ruthless occupation. Apparently you couldn't after all." Emma eyed her as if she were x-raying her soul.

"I still remember the day you came from your aunt and uncle's to live with Abigail. You were a tiny, lost child with a pink backpack, clutching a teddy bear with a red scarf and one missing ear. Your eyes were so big that they took up most of your face."

Catherine glanced at Will, unsure if she was ready to have him hear this, but most likely he'd heard it all from Gram. "Yes. Initially I'd stayed with my mother's sister, Ellen, and her husband, Max."

"But your grandmother never liked it much. She told me that Ellen and Max were too…what was the word?" Emma looked around to make sure they weren't within hearing distance. "They were too *restless* to have a child. I never really understood what she meant by that."

Catherine, however, understood perfectly. "Max and Ellen are entrepreneurs. They love to travel. Max does business all over the world and Ellen accompanies him. It's an opportunity for Ellen to take photos across the continents. She's built up a fairly serious reputation as a photographer. By choice, they've never had children."

"It's probably for the best if they couldn't stay home," Emma said, her tone disapproving. "Children need a stable environment."

"That's what my grandmother thought, too." Catherine ran her fingers through her hair. She'd given thanks to God countless times that her grandmother had held fast and insisted on legal custody. Even now, today, she and her aunt were on opposite ends of the spectrum. The conversation they'd just had was proof of that.

Catherine shrugged. "It all worked out, I guess. It's probably the reason that I specialized in family law."

"More than worked out. It seems to me it was a big success." Will glanced at Emma. "This gives me hope."

Emma nodded in understanding, leaving Catherine in the dark as to what they were talking about.

Before she could ask him what he meant, a bear of a man bore down on them and Catherine threw out her arms. "Jerry!" At that moment he picked her off her feet and gathered her into his arms.

Will and Emma backed away as Catherine greeted her old friend.

Will watched Catherine talk to the newcomer with sudden animation and felt oddly protective. She was spectacularly beautiful, in a tense, agitated kind of way. Will couldn't fault her for being a bundle of nerves. Losing Abigail had knocked him for a loop and he couldn't imagine how it might be for Catherine.

She was too thin, and her high cheekbones were more prominent than they might have been had she been carrying another ten or fifteen pounds. For some odd reason, he had an urgent desire to cook for her. Perhaps because he couldn't think of another thing to do for this woman whose suffering was written across her face.

He rarely felt helpless. Having lived and seen a lot of life had taught him to survive. He was confident about most things he faced, but Catherine was something else. Like his late friend and mentor, Abigail, he was rarely wrong about someone's character. Beneath her shell of self-sufficiency, Catherine Stanhope was fragile and vulnerable.

Emma, who was acting as hostess, flitted over to him. "She reminds you of Abigail, doesn't she? Independent, smart, self-reliant…." Emma made a tsk-tsking noise with her tongue. "She was even more so before…" Her voice trailed away.

"Before what?"

"I'm not quite sure. But I do know something has changed her. Abigail told me that a case had affected Catherine deeply and she was having a hard time getting over it. Catherine's always been very open and forthright, but she has walls up now. I can't explain it, but it feels as if she holds people at bay sometimes."

He tensed involuntarily. He preferred people who were honest, not guarded or secretive.

"I know this has been hard on you, Will." Her grandmotherly concern was evident. "You and Abigail were very close. She loved you like a son. I'm sorry for your loss, as well. Are you okay?"

"I must admit I'm a little poleaxed by what's happened, but I'll be fine." He drew himself to his full six-foot-two height and rolled his shoulders to relax them before giving Emma a lopsided grin. "Which reminds me, I'd better go find Charley before he gets into some mischief."

"That's a darling boy you have."

Will didn't comment. His mind was too busy digesting the fact that not only was Catherine an attorney, but that she had been at the center of a custody case as a child. Could she help him with the problem that was currently knocking at his door? And of course there was the even bigger question. Would she?

Chapter Three

Catherine gazed up at her old high-school class-mate, Jerry Travers. He was a big teddy bear in a bow tie.

"Catherine, I'm so sorry about your grandmother."

"Thanks, Jerry. I appreciate everyone's kindness. How's life going for you?"

"Same old, same old. Deeds, contracts, wills, estate planning and, fortunately, very few criminal cases. That's the blessing of practicing in Pleasant. Most of the work is, well, pretty pleasant."

She couldn't help smiling back at him.

"I'm busier than I used to be, of course," Jerry added.

"You are?" She studied his profile, the prominent nose, strong chin and high forehead. He looked little different than he had in high school.

"Dad is trying to retire. Emphasis on 'trying.' He'll never give up practicing law altogether, but he does need to cut back. He had a minor heart attack last winter and my mother is adamant about getting him to slow down. I'm trying to carry a bigger load and make it look like it's easy so that he'll get the idea he can take a few days off here and there." He took a sandwich off a tray someone brought by. "How about you? How's the legal profession treating you?"

"I resigned from my job."

"No kidding?" His dark brows raised with astonishment. "I thought you had some peach of a career on tap…at least that's what your grandmother always said."

"I suppose I did, but I needed a break," Catherine responded vaguely. She wasn't ready to go into detail about her life choices quite yet.

"How long will you be staying in Pleasant?"

"Probably several weeks. My time is my own right now."

"Abigail always hoped you'd come back here, you know."

Surprise rippled through her. "To practice law? What about the esteemed firm of Travers & Travers?"

Jerry chuckled. "Oh, them. More than once Abigail asked Dad if he'd hire you if you came home."

"She did?" Catherine was taken aback. Her

grandmother had had dreams for her she'd never voiced. What else didn't she know?

"Dad always said yes, of course."

"To pacify her, no doubt."

"Not really. I believe he meant it." Jerry turned an appraising eye on her. "He probably still would. My mother would be eternally grateful. If Dad thought he had a competent attorney in the office other than me, he might ease up finally."

"It sounds like you're trying to offer me a job," Catherine said lightly. It was odd that right after she'd quit her job, other opportunities began to appear.

"Are you looking for one?"

"I'm considering doing some teaching. Of course, that was before Gram died."

"You'd be good at it. You'd be good at anything you tried, Catherine. I know you've got your plate full right now. All I'm saying is that if you want to do some part-time work while you're deciding your next step, Travers & Travers might be able to accommodate you. I saw you argue a case in the Cities, if you remember. I was very impressed by your skill and confidence. You left everyone else in the dust."

"That's very kind of you, Jerry…"

The big man snorted. "It's not kind at all, Catherine. You're one of the best. You'd be doing us a kindness by representing our firm."

Jerry backed away when someone from the dining room called her name. "It's great to see you again, Catherine. I'm so sorry about the circumstances. No pressure about my offer. I just wanted you to know that if time gets heavy on your hands, you have an option."

"I appreciate the offer. I just…" She didn't even get time to finish her sentence before another friend of Abigail took her arm and pulled her away.

When the last guest said goodbye, Catherine dropped into the nearest chair with a groan.

Emma patted her hand. "You've had enough for one day, dear. You're white as a sheet. Why don't you come back to my house tonight so you can get a good night's sleep? I know you'd planned to stay at Hope House, but you can check out the place just as well in the morning."

"I haven't walked the grounds or been upstairs," Catherine protested without much enthusiasm. "I really should…"

"Nothing will change overnight. It will all be here for you tomorrow."

Suddenly, spending the night here felt like a very bad idea. Here at Hope House Catherine knew she would do nothing but think about what she'd lost, when all she really wanted was to fall into a deep, dreamless sleep.

"I'll take you up on that, Emma."

She knew she'd be asleep before her head hit the pillow.

Catherine awoke slowly, the light of the sun filtering through the thick lace curtains and across her bed. She lay on her back thinking of the remarkable ceiling in her own bedroom at Hope House, which had been decorated with plaster swirls that had been piped on like frosting on a wedding cake. She'd taken the house for granted as a child, but its remarkable features struck her now. Although Emma's home was lovely, it was a pale comparison to Hope House. Catherine had been living in a fairy-tale house back then and hadn't even noticed. It would be painful to go back there without Abigail, but it had to be done.

Her limbs felt heavy and it took her some time to roll to her side and put her feet on the pink-and-blue Aubusson rug on the floor beside the bed. Gently she raised and lowered her shoulders and moved her head from side to side. Once her blood was flowing, she stretched broadly and stood up. Her body felt as if it had been beaten as her tense muscles screamed in protest.

After a quick shower, Catherine grabbed clothing from her bag and padded downstairs barefoot to find Emma in the kitchen whipping up a batch of pancakes. Coffee was brewed and fresh-squeezed orange juice was already on the table.

"You have no idea how much I appreciate this, Emma." Catherine poured herself some coffee. "I couldn't bear the thought of sleeping in the big house alone last night."

"It's the least I can do, sweet girl. I hope you slept well."

"Quite soundly. I suppose being exhausted from getting ready to move and then the tension of yesterday wore me out."

"People always sleep better in Pleasant," Emma said complacently. "No bright streetlights except a couple on Main Street and a street corner here and there, no traffic noise, no airplanes arriving and taking off, and all the gorgeous, mature trees— it's like a cocoon, protected from the rest of the world."

"I appreciate that, I…"

A knock on the door interrupted the conversation. Will Tanner strode in, dark hair still damp and curling from the shower, a night's growth of beard shadowing his jawline. "Good morning, ladies. How are things today?" His gaze went directly to Catherine.

She looked as if she'd lost ten pounds overnight, he observed. Her cheeks were hollow and there were dark smudges beneath her eyes. She sat at the kitchen table in well-washed jeans that had seen better years and a simple white T-shirt. Her long blond hair was pulled back into a ponytail that made her look like a teenager. She'd tucked her feet beneath her and held a large coffee mug in her hands. She lifted it to her face to inhale the aroma and breathed deeply.

Will had never wanted to rescue someone from sadness so badly in his life. Except Charley, of course, but Charley was family. His sister Annie's blood ran in his veins.

"Morning, Will. I thought you'd be by." Emma held up a carafe. "Coffee?"

"Don't mind if I do." Maybe a jolt of caffeine would take the edge off his fuzziness. He'd dreamed all night of Abigail and the plans they'd had together.

In the dream he and Abigail sat at her kitchen table as they always did, discussing the house and the forever-growing list of restoration projects he was to tackle.

"Will," she would say, "promise me that whatever happens, you'll finish this house." Her expression was intent. "Don't get itchy feet. Please say that you'll stay here until it's done."

"Abigail, there's no reason for me to leave you. The house will be done. I promise. I'm not a quitter."

"Refurbishing this house is my gift to the

Stanhope family. I married my husband, Charles, as a very young woman and it changed everything about my life." Abigail's eyes would flash with resolve and she'd squeeze his hand so tightly that it almost hurt.

Then she'd stare straight into his eyes and say, "The Stanhopes were generous to a fault. They helped to mold me into who I am today. I will be forever grateful for the way they took me in as a true daughter. And they loved Hope House, as I grew to."

He was ready to reassure her again that he wasn't planning to go anywhere when he woke and realized that Abigail was gone. By dawn he knew with complete certainty what he had to do. She'd given him not only a job but a place to live—a cozy apartment in the guesthouse, a stable home for his nephew, Charley, and as a result, a renewed purpose for his life. If ever he was to claim Charley as his own son, a real home was imperative. The town was safe, idyllic and friendly, perfect for a growing child, and their place was small but comfortable— no matter what his sister-in-law thought. He was tired of continually locking horns with Sheila on the matter. He *had* to restore the house as Abigail had asked. It was imperative that he make a home for his little boy.

Then an unsettling thought occurred to him. What had Abigail told her granddaughter of her plans? Catherine owned the house now. She could sell it or turn it into a gift shop or any fool thing she wanted.

Still, even in death, Abigail was a force to be reckoned with. He would do what he'd promised her.

He looked up to see Emma and Catherine staring at him expectantly. How long had his mind drifted?

"Sorry. I didn't sleep very well last night." He looked at Catherine. "Did you?"

"I think it felt less like sleep and more like a coma," she admitted. "I was already on my way to Pleasant for some badly needed R&R..." As she said it, she looked troubled.

There was more to this woman than met the eye, Will sensed. He hoped he'd get to know her well enough to learn what made her tick.

Catherine felt uncomfortable beneath Will's intent gaze. "Tell me more about what you did for Gram," she suggested.

"I'm doing a lot of carpentry work right now, as you probably already know. It was your grandmother's dream that Hope House be preserved for posterity. I've been helping her restore the place."

No, she didn't know. Catherine couldn't recall her grandmother saying that to her. Of course, Gram had traveled to Minneapolis for their visits and Hope House was rarely a topic of conversation.

Now she knew why he seemed so at ease in this house. There was a time when she felt she was Abigail's primary confidant. Will had been here for Gram and she hadn't. She'd trade it all for an hour with her now.

"I live in the guesthouse," he added as if it were an afterthought.

Catherine blinked. Gram hadn't mentioned that either.

"I'm a relatively recent addition to the property." Tanner looked amused by her surprise. "Six months, remember? Living in the guesthouse is part of my payment for my work. Abigail and I struck a deal."

What exactly did that mean?

He thrust his hands into his pockets. "It was my understanding that she was going to surprise you when you arrived. From what I gathered, Abigail was sure you'd be pleased because you'd grown up here and your family home had so much history."

He gave her a shrewd stare. "She thought you felt the same way about Hope House that she did."

Will might as well have pounded a stake into her heart. Of course she loved Hope House! But her life was very different from Gram's. What's more, she'd been away from home except for summer breaks and visits since she was eighteen years old. She loved Pleasant and Hope House, but it was part of her past, not her future. Maybe it was a good thing that Gram hadn't understood that. It might have hurt her to know they weren't on the same page.

"How did you and my grandmother meet?"

"Through my cousin, who reroofed the house a year ago. She called him when she was looking for help with the renovating and he suggested me. I went uptown for supplies. I'm on my way to Hope House to work right now," Will said. "Do you want to come back with me?"

"I'd like that. I'll be right back." She could feel Will and Emma watching her as she left the kitchen. It was as if they were worried about her. Especially Will.

That was puzzling. She'd just met the man and knew very little about him other than he was a very handsome man. And, of course, Abigail had liked him. She hoped Gram was right to put her faith in him.

She returned wearing the same jeans and T-shirt with a powder-blue sweatshirt. She'd pulled her long tumble of hair into a knot at the base of her neck. On her feet was a pair of her favorite flip-flops.

It occurred to her that for the first time in months she felt free.

No power suit and low-heeled pumps today. No arm-taxing briefcase full of legal papers, no court dates, no judges or bailiffs and no guards at courthouse security. And no way to mess up someone's life. She was free. Even the tragedy of the moment couldn't erase the relief she felt.

When she reached the bottom of the stairs, she said, "Sorry I'm so casual today."

"Don't apologize. You're a beautiful woman, Catherine. Most ladies would give anything to look like you." Then, to her delight, he blushed.

Catherine kept her eye on him as they said good-bye to Emma and crawled into his pickup truck. He was extremely appealing, with that day-old growth of stubble on his cheeks. His dark hair was thick and rumpled and his eyebrows dark and straight over his remarkable eyes. He was tall and leanly muscled, dark-eyed and exuded an aura of strength—both physical and mental. No wonder her grandmother had been so cavalier when Catherine had asked about work around the house. Will had been her secret weapon against quickly growing grass and wood decay.

The thoughts of her grandmother brought tears to her eyes again. Abigail had been her entire family. Her absent aunt and uncle hardly counted. It was all gone now—Gram, her job, her condo…. Only Hope House remained to be dealt with.

This was a fresh start, something she'd been wanting for a long time. She was eager to take on a new opportunity but not when she was feeling guilty about it. About selling Hope House.

Pleasant was just what its name implied. As they

drove down Main Street, Catherine watched the picturesque storefronts go by. The Nook, part gift shop and part quilt shop, had a colorful banner flying from the eaves that announced a sale. Across the street was an antiques store called Becky's Attic, which was owned by a high-school friend of Catherine. Because it was near lake country, Pleasant had a steady flow of visitors all summer long that supported the shops and during long winters for ice fishing and sledding. A feeling of stillness washed over her as she viewed the unchanging storefronts and recalled shopkeepers who had been behind their counters since she was a child.

She also had a growing awareness of the man beside her. His physical presence was compelling.

"Nice, isn't it?"

"There are a lot of memories for me here," she said softly as she shifted more closely to the truck door. Her attraction to him was disconcerting.

"Good ones, I hope."

"Very." She studied his profile as he drove. There was gentleness about his features that surprised her. She liked it. Maybe she was too accustomed to hard-edged attorneys. Even if her coworkers had had soft sides, they tried never to let them show.

"You're lucky—about the good memories, I mean. I would have given anything to have grown up in a place like this." He said it so emphatically that she stared at him quizzically.

"This is a perfect place for a child," he explained. "He can have freedom to roam and yet enough people watching out for him that he can't get into much trouble. You know that stuff about it taking a village to raise a kid? This is that kind of place."

"A kid like you were?"

"Me? No. I was a little wildcat according to everyone who knew me. It would have taken an entire metropolis to do much with me. I was thinking about my nephew, Charley." He smiled slightly. "You met him yesterday."

"Ah, yes, the one who threw a dump truck on top of me."

"Charley lives with me now, although my brother and sister-in-law would like to change that. His mom, my sister, Annie, had cirrhosis. She died about five months ago."

"I'm so sorry for your loss."

He looked pained. "It was difficult to watch someone throw her life away, but my sister couldn't quit drinking." He strained to get the words out, as if he didn't want to talk about this but couldn't help himself. "Charley had a tough life growing up with an alcoholic mom. My sister loved him, but she couldn't keep her act together, even for him."

They pulled into the driveway of Hope House before she could respond. Today she looked—really looked—at the yard and gardens. The lawns were lush green carpets, so soft-looking she yearned to walk over them barefoot. Not a leaf or a twig marred the expanse. The variegated hostas had tripled in size since her last visit and the beds of moss roses were bright and colorful as bags of jelly beans. What had this man put the plants and grass on? Steroids?

"The yard is spectacular. You've done an amazing job with the whole place." The old porch swing she'd loved as a child had been restored and was piled high with yellow, blue and white floral pillows. Even the white wicker furniture, which had been hidden away in the storage shed, was now inviting instead of decrepit. "It's as if you gave the whole place a facelift. I could really enjoy this spot if…" She paused.

"If your grandmother were here to enjoy it with you?" he asked perceptively.

"Yes."

"If it's any comfort to you, your grandmother *is* here. She walked me through every decision and every repair she wanted me to make. This place *is* Abigail."

That wasn't exactly what she wanted to hear.

But the house wasn't all she had of Gram, Catherine reminded herself. Abigail was still alive in her heart after all, and wasn't that where it counted most? Surely she didn't have to own Hope House to keep Gram's memory alive.

Chapter Four

On the way past the mailbox, Will plucked the daily paper out of the cubby designated for the news. Then he reached into his pocket and pulled out a key ring and opened the front door with a familiar hand. If she hadn't known better, she might have thought *he* was the owner of this house.

But inside, the house fairly crackled with her grandmother's personality. It felt even more so today without all the people milling about.

Abigail Stanhope was colorful and her taste eclectic. There were original oils by American artists hung next to Catherine's handprint from first grade and a collage of leaves she'd collected for a science class. Abigail had made sure their frames were every bit as elaborate and prominently displayed as the other paintings.

Tearing up, Catherine turned quickly away only to run face-first into Will's warm, broad chest. He smelled like fresh air and wood shavings, a surprisingly pleasant combination. His compelling brown eyes flecked with gold were kind, compassionate and questioning.

"I'm so sorry." She backed away from him, the stranger who, for some reason, didn't feel like a stranger at all. "Thank you for bringing me home...." Even though it didn't feel much like home without Gram present.

At that moment the front door opened and Charley raced in. "I saw you from Mikey's house. His mom said I could come over as long as you were here." He slipped his hand into Will's. "Is it okay, Uncle Will?"

The expression of unadulterated love on Will's face made Catherine's own heart race. *This,* she thought, was how a child needed to be loved.

"Sure, kiddo, but you have to find a way to entertain yourself while I show Ms. Stanhope what Abigail and I have been up to."

Will saw to it that Charley was ensconced with the box of toys Abigail kept there for him, then he beckoned her toward the stairs. "We started up here."

She followed him up the long curving arc of the stairs, curious to see what her grandmother had hatched with this guy. A little paint, probably, and some new light fixtures. It was unrealistic to hope he'd repaired the claw-footed cast-iron tub in the hallway bath. The porcelain had been chipped ever since she was a child…and those awful, sticking windows…

When she got to the top of the stairs, Catherine stopped dead in her tracks. Jaw gaping, she stared at the chaotic mess before her.

Two-by-fours lined one side of a hall partially blocked by a table saw. There was a black, gaping hole in the plaster at chest height, and that old monster of a claw-footed tub was sitting upside down in the hall like an upended turtle.

"Watch your step. It's a little crowded in here right now. As soon as the tub restorers come to pick it up, we'll be able to maneuver better. I needed it out so I could tear up the bathroom floor."

She glanced, horrified, at the gaping hole in the hallway wall. "Tear it up? Haven't you done enough damage already?"

"You have to make things worse to make them better," he said cheerfully. "The wood is soft around the tub from a leak. I'm replumbing, too. Those pipes are showing their age. Remodeling and restoration are always a mess, but when the results are good, it's worth it. Sometimes life works out that way, too, you know. You think you're in a real mess and it turns out to be the best thing for you."

"If that's the case, 'better' should be right around the corner for me," Catherine muttered. She couldn't imagine things getting much worse. She pointed at the maw in the wall. "What on earth have you done there?"

He looked insulted that she'd had to ask. "I'm putting the dumbwaiter back where it belongs."

"What dumbwaiter?"

"The one that was in the house originally and was likely removed before you were born. The pulleys are still in the wall. I've got the architects' original blueprints and I'm restoring things to their previous condition."

Catherine looked around, stunned. "This will take forever to put back together!"

"Abigail gave me as much time as I needed to finish this. I figure a couple years, at least. That's how long the lease runs on the guesthouse, too. We planned it that way."

Catherine sat down on an overturned bucket. A splash of cold reality hit her. What had Gram been thinking, committing to him and to this project for that long? She hadn't been thinking about dying, that was for sure.

But things had changed radically. Catherine didn't want to be the bad guy, that was the very thing she'd thought she'd left behind with her career as an attorney. But she didn't need this monster of a house once she decided how to move on with her life. Unfortunately, if she decided not to keep the house, it meant that she would have to fire Will Tanner and break the lease on the guesthouse.

But for now it was a moot question. This place couldn't be sold now anyway, not in this condition. Any potential buyer would run screaming in the other direction the way the house's second floor looked. She gazed at the wreckage. Will needed to put this house back together ASAP. It had to be done before she could move on with her life. That meant the sooner the better.

Obviously Catherine and Abigail hadn't discussed the house much at all, Will thought. And from the look of it, the house was much more Abigail's passion than her granddaughter's. Still, Catherine looked as if she'd been slapped with a paintbrush when she'd seen the hall. And she'd never even heard about the dumbwaiter. Maybe that was a conversation Abigail had saved for him. They'd certainly spent enough hours talking about the house and their other favorite topics—God, faith and salvation.

Abigail had been the one to introduce him to Christ. She'd said He was her best friend and would be his, too. Will was in need of a friend right then, with his sister dying, Charley wandering around like a lost waif and his own brother and sister-in-law questioning his ability to raise the boy.

Faith was what had ultimately gotten him through Annie's passing. Better yet, before she died, Annie had accepted Christ as her Savior, as well. The peace of knowing that was enormous for Will. It hadn't been easy, her dying, but at least he knew they'd meet again. And she'd be free of the addiction that had haunted her.

Until he'd met Abigail, he'd known little about Christianity except what he'd read on signs outside of churches. Now it was alive to him and it had breathed new life into his soul. He couldn't believe the blessing sometimes. Will felt humbled and grateful every day for his heavenly inheritance—and for Abigail, who'd pointed him in the right direction.

Then he glanced at Catherine. She was looking small and vulnerable in the wide, high-ceilinged hall. From the moment he'd met her he'd felt a little off-kilter.

She certainly wasn't Abigail. She was considerably more reserved, almost cool, and didn't seem nearly as impressed as he'd hoped with the work they'd done. Some sort of affirmation would be nice—or was it reassurance he wanted? Now that Charley had come to live with him, he was determined to provide the child with the home he'd been missing. Will wanted nothing more than to put down roots for a few years in the guesthouse. This sad but beautiful woman held the reins now. Could he trust her to do the right thing? He didn't want to believe she'd stand in his way or suggest he leave the guest cottage... Surely not!

"I also tore out part of the wall in this bedroom," he said, more to fill the silence than anything.

Catherine poked her nose into the wrecked and dusty space. "Why on earth would you tear out the wall of my bedroom?" The furniture was covered with tarps.

"Originally this was the master bedroom." Will stepped into the room and began gesticulating with his hands. "Back in those days, however, the master suite was often made up of two adjoining rooms with a door or even a dressing room between them. The larger of the two rooms was where the woman of the house slept and her husband slept next door in the smaller room."

"No kidding? I didn't know that."

"We checked some diaries Abigail found and we think that was the arrangement Obadiah and his wife had. Abigail wants…wanted…me to put the door back in so it is like the suite it was."

He scowled a little, which did nothing to harm his looks. "I don't know why people thought that was such a good idea. What's the use of being married if you live in separate spaces? That's an idea I'm glad we improved on."

Catherine left Will and hurried downstairs to gather her thoughts. The house, the mess, Abigail's wishes and her own confusion made her head spin. At the bottom of the steps she nearly tripped over a small army of soldiers assembled on the hand-tied silk foyer rug.

"Be careful, lady," a small voice piped. "You're knocking down the rebel army!"

She avoided as many of the rebels as she could but came down hard on a miniature cannon, twisting her ankle. To catch herself, Catherine reached for the nearest thing available, a free-standing coat-rack where one of Gram's straw hats hung. It and Catherine both teetered for a moment before falling into an ungainly pile right on top of the entire defending militia.

Miniature sabers and rifles poked into Catherine like needles, and as she rolled away to escape them, she managed only to embed herself on the rebel camp. Some of these soldiers were metal instead of plastic, and she felt as if she were rolling around on a bed of prickly jacks, the kind she'd played with as a child. "Ouch!"

"Kaboom!" Charley roared happily. "And a meteorite from Planet Zeus landed on them all, crushing the rebellion and killing a whole bunch of dinosaurs besides. Double kaboom!"

Then a small face with brown eyes, rosy cheeks and a fringe of dark hair appeared over her. "Are you okay, lady? You made a great meteorite." The cherubic-looking little boy frowned. "But I think you broke the rifles off a bunch of my men."

Then he brightened. "They need to go to the… the…." He looked quizzically at Catherine.

"The infirmary?" she suggested, struggling to keep a straight face. This was one cute, huggable kid.

"Yeah, that's it. The in-fur-mary." He scooped up a handful of the injured and swept them into a basket. Making a passable sound as an ambulance siren, he raced out of the room.

Catherine turned to the sound of pounding footsteps on the stairs and soon it was Will's concerned face that peered down at her. "Are you hurt?"

"Not so much that I have to go to the in-fur-mary," she said, struggling to her feet.

Will reached out a hand to help her but turned his head toward the back of the house. "Charley, you get in here and apologize to Ms. Stanhope right now!"

Silence.

"If you don't, these toy soldiers are going MIA, *now*," Will ordered in a passable chief commander's voice.

A squeak in the floor was the only sound of movement. Catherine got to her feet, wiped off a couple plastic soldiers that had imbedded themselves in the folds of her shirt, and waited.

Charley's tousled head peeked around the corner of the dining-room door. His cheeks were flushed and his eyes danced despite the inevitable scolding that was about to come.

Catherine fought her urge to smile.

Will seemed to have no such trouble. He was fuming. "Please come over here and apologize. I told you not to set up camp where you'd be in the way."

"I didn't think anyone would mind now that Gram isn't here," the child said, looking repentant.

Gram? There he was again, referring to Abigail as his grandmother.

Charley scuffed the soles of his battered tennis shoes on the highly polished floor. "I'm sorry, lady. I didn't mean to trip you. I'll pick 'em up and take them outside."

Will put his hand on the boy's shoulder. "Charley, did you know that Ms. Stanhope owns this house now?"

The child's eyes grew wide. "Gram gave it to you? You're lucky…"

Catherine expected him to add "so now you much be rich" or some other childish leap of logic.

Instead he added, "…because you're Gram's real granddaughter. You're not like me. I'm just her pretend grandson." Longing filled his eyes.

Her heart melted in her chest at the child's earnest statement. "Thank's for reminding me of that. I had Abigail as my gram for a long time." She reached out to touch the boy's silken hair. "You're a very sweet boy, Charley. Thank you."

Will cleared his throat. "Charley, get this mess out of sight, will you? You can set up in the kitchen." As Charley busied himself on the floor, Will took Catherine's arm and led her into the sunroom off the main living room.

"Are you okay? Any puncture wounds from your battle with the soldiers?"

When she shook her head, he continued. "You'll have to excuse Charley. He and Abigail really clicked when he came to live with me. He asked her if he could call her 'Grandma,' but she told him her favorite grandchild in the whole world called her 'Gram' and that he should, too. He has the same first name as her husband and she liked that. I hope you don't mind."

Mind? How could she mind an orphaned child, a child like she had been, seeking love?

"Charley came to me so eager for affection and Abigail liked having a child in the house. Frankly, Charley was fascinated with Abigail, and I took advantage of the fact. With his mother gone, Charley hasn't had many women in his life and he adored her."

"That's fine, Will. He's adorable. In fact he…"

She'd almost said "looks a lot like you," but stopped herself.

She didn't even want to hint at the fact that Charley's uncle was pretty adorable himself.

Chapter Five

The next morning the phone rang before Will had had his first cup of coffee. That alone was ominous.

"Hello?" he growled into the phone, hoping to frighten off whoever was calling.

No such luck. His sister-in-law Sheila's voice came across the line. "How's Charley?"

"Fine. Just like he was yesterday—and the day before."

Will had to keep reminding himself that Sheila cared about Charley, too, even though she was making life miserable for everyone else. Maybe if she'd had a few kids of her own, she wouldn't be so dead set on having Charley. But Charley wasn't a toy for Sheila to play mother over…. Will reeled at that uncharitable thought. Maybe the reason he couldn't understand Sheila was that she was a woman with a biological clock that seemed to have sputtered to a stop. Patiently he began to explain Charley's day to Sheila, as she demanded to hear.

Later, Will glanced out the window of the mansion's upstairs bathroom where he'd spent the past hour tearing out rotted flooring and his jaw dropped. Coming up the sidewalk was Catherine Stanhope. She was dressed in hiking shorts, a white T-shirt and tennis shoes. Catherine carried a lunch bucket and looked like one of the employees he managed on his construction crew—only prettier. Her expression was uneasy but determined, as if she were a round peg planning to insert herself into a square hole.

He suppressed a smile. That look of determination was one he'd seen on Abigail's face quite regularly in the past weeks, ever since she'd made her final decisions as to what she would do with the house. Nothing and no one could get in her way when she wore that expression, and Will had a hunch that Abigail's granddaughter was cut out of the same cloth. He hoped that he and Catherine would agree on the plans for the house. He didn't care to butt heads with another force of nature like Abigail.

He was weary of women who didn't understand his perspective—like his sister-in-law. Before Sheila had hung up this morning she had again harangued him about the fact that Charley was living with him instead of her and his brother, Matt, just as she had ever since Annie's death.

To hear Sheila tell it, Will was utterly inept and ill suited to raise Charley. Sheila demanded custody of the boy, saying it was a travesty that the child didn't have two proper parents—like her and her husband. Will didn't consider Sheila a suitable parent. She was more like an absentee landlord.

They called him restless and a wanderer, which might have been true a few years ago, but now he was willing to be as rooted as a giant oak to keep his nephew with him.

Catherine, a big-time attorney, had practically landed on their doorstep, he thought. Maybe she could help him keep Charley. It had, at least, given him a sliver of hope.

Dream on. It's never going to happen. She doesn't have to bother with the likes of us. His fantasy was just that, a pipe dream. He redoubled his efforts on the floor.

Wood splinters flew as he worked and the squeal of nails releasing from old flooring filled his ears. It felt good to use his body rather than his mind. One of the things that he had found as a new Christian was the struggle to turn his concerns over to God and to leave them there.

"Trust Him, Will," he could still hear Abigail say. "If you don't trust Him, do you really believe in Him? Each time you experience a prayer answered, you'll see His faithfulness and your trust will grow. Mark my words."

Warm with exertion, Will wiped his forehead on the sleeve of his denim work shirt. He hadn't needed to work out since he'd come to Abigail's. She kept him so busy lifting, toting and digging that half the time he felt like begging for mercy.

He tested another board with the toe of his foot and grimaced. Another soft spot. That made it certain that the entire floor would have to go. He took a crowbar, wedged the flattened end beneath the end of the board and pried it loose. The visitor he'd spied out the window was forgotten for the moment.

The grating sounds emanating from the main bath made Catherine wince. It sounded more as if the man was tearing the house down than restoring it. It was a good thing she was here to oversee things and keep Tanner in line.

She smiled a little. The idea of someone like her keeping up with a powerful man like Tanner bordered on the ludicrous. Still, a big boat could be guided by a little rudder. That's what she would have to be. Bigger didn't have to be better.

She put the lunch bucket Emma had packed on the chair by the front door, mounted the steps to the second floor and followed the loud banging noises. What she found nearly took her breath away.

Will Tanner, wearing a T-shirt, denim jeans and a tool belt, was balancing precariously on the floor joists that had held the wooden floorboards in place. Beneath was the plaster that formed the ceiling of the room below. One misstep and Tanner would land in the sunroom downstairs.

He looked up and grinned at her. "Good morning. How did you sleep?"

"Fine, thank you. Could you please come over here where there's a floor to stand on?" Even in her dismay Catherine couldn't miss the sight of Will's strong, well-built frame.

He bounced a little on the tips of his toes. "There's something to stand on here."

She reached out as if to stop him and nearly lost her own footing.

"Don't worry. I'm accustomed to this." He walked across the joists like a cat and stopped beside her. "Piece of cake. You don't have to look so concerned. I do this for a living, you know."

She was surprised at the nervous feeling in her stomach. "When will you start to lay the new floor?" By the look of it, the house would never come back together.

"Tomorrow afternoon, I think. Or the first thing the day after. Why?"

"Oh, no particular reason," she said vaguely. "For now, is there anything I can do to help?"

The pressure on her felt greater because she'd

recently been getting emails from the law school about faculty gatherings, workshops and the like. Although, because she would be part-time at first, she wasn't duty-bound to attend any of them, she felt it would be a nice gesture. Even more, it would be a true step toward that other life she was seeking.

"I cut a hole in the wall in the bedroom. I'd like to get that door put in between the rooms as soon as possible."

"Maybe I could help with that?"

He gave her a startled look but led her into the bedroom that had once been hers. "I don't think I explained what I was planning last night. I found the studs in the walls, marked the position of the door and cut out the hole, but I haven't taken down the plaster yet. You could do that. I don't even have to put up a new header for the door because the original one is still there…."

Catherine had no idea what he was talking about. Her education had been broad and varied, but there'd been little opportunity to learn carpentry and construction.

"There are hammers and crowbars in the hall. Help yourself."

And before she could say anything, Tanner strode out of the room.

Well, then…. She picked up a hammer and took a swing at the wall where he had marked the outline of the doorway. There was a satisfying crunch and chips of plaster flew. She hit it again, harder, this time. It was surprisingly therapeutic, as if the tension and grief she'd been carrying left her body, exploded out the head of the hammer and fell to the floor with the chunks and crumbles of plaster. She swung fiercely at the wall as a refrain formed in her mind. She took a swing for the Three C's and all the stress and pressure the firm had provided her over the years. She took another swing for that dreadful woman who had lied to her about wanting custody of her son and one for the manipulation and deceit. One cathartic swing was for herself for so foolishly buying into that story. How naive could she have been? And take that, death, for stealing my grandmother away....

The hammering on the other side of the wall was unrelenting, Will noted. Catherine was really tearing into it. Too bad he hadn't had her on his crew when he was running demolition jobs. By the rhythmic sound of her swings, she was a miniature wrecking ball in action. Good. That freed him to work on other things. What's more, it would keep her busy and out of his hair.

Lovely as she was, he didn't need her underfoot right now. She'd tire of this soon enough and move on, but for now this would keep her occupied. Will turned up the radio he'd brought from home and lost himself in the nasal twangs of Hank Williams, country-western-style loneliness, cheating hearts and lovesick blues.

It was the faltering rhythm of the pounding next door that finally jarred him back to the present. How long had Catherine been at it? He'd lost all track of time. Then he heard a groan and the clatter of something falling to the floor. He was swiftly on his feet and bolted into the adjoining room.

Catherine sat on the floor in a pile of plaster rubble. Long strands of her golden hair had fallen out of the rubber binder with which she'd held it back and perspiration beaded on her forehead. The plaster dust in the air made her look as if she'd been powdered in flour, and specks of it clung to her face and arms. When she looked up at Will, it was with weariness and—relief?—on her face.

"Are you all right?" He kneeled beside her. "I lost track of time. You've been in here working for a while."

"I'm going to feel it tomorrow," she predicted, rubbing her shoulder, "but it was therapeutic. I'm not accustomed to physically working out issues. It felt good to imagine that wall as everything that's been going wrong lately." She guiltily glanced at the wall. "I guess I had more to work out than even I thought."

For the first time, Will took his eyes off Catherine. He groaned mentally as he took in the wreckage. She'd hammered out the plaster inside the designated lines, all right—and everything outside them in a three-foot radius, as well. Nearly a third of the wall was either missing or cracked beyond repair.

"I guess I got carried away and went overboard," Catherine said, her voice small. "I forgot to hammer inside the lines."

Will took a deep breath, giving him time to think and to ensure that he wouldn't say something he might regret. "You certainly did," he finally managed. "Now, instead of putting a regular door between the rooms, we can install a patio door."

"Did I ruin it?" She looked as though she were about to cry. "I just kept swinging and swinging...."

"It's nothing that a little lath and a few coats of plaster won't fix." He didn't go into the patience he'd need to do a satisfactory job of it. "Piece of cake," he added faintly. He also didn't add that it would no doubt add even more time to the project.

"Oh, good." She looked relieved. "I'm glad I could help."

Will closed his eyes briefly. With help like hers, he'd be lucky to get this project done before he was eligible for Social Security.

"Anyone who works as hard as you do deserves a break," he said gently. She was much too fragile to hear just how much trouble she'd made for him. "How about lunch?"

* * *

He really was very sweet, Catherine thought as she looked over Will's shoulder at the bedroom wall. She was genuinely glad to help him out—and would have been pleased to do so even if she didn't want the house project wrapped up quickly.

"Emma sent me here with a lunch for two. Want to join me?"

"Are you kidding? I never turn down Emma's cooking." He looked around the dusty room. "We can eat on the patio."

They trooped downstairs and Catherine grabbed the lunch box and followed Will out the back door to the stone terrace at the bottom of the stairs. She'd helped Gram pick out the wrought-iron furniture for this spot, and the bright red cushions. Would everything here always remind her of Gram? Probably.

After they had eaten they sat, not speaking, soaking up the sun and watching hummingbirds sip the nectar from the flowers in a massive planter nearby. Catherine felt better than she had in days. Perhaps now was the time to ask Will some of the questions she'd been entertaining.

Before she could say anything, Will stood up to his full height and held out his hand to her.

"Want to take a walk?" he suggested. "I'd like you to see the rose beds. Abigail had to teach me how to grow them, but I think they're doing well."

She slipped her small hand into his larger one and allowed him to pull her up.

"We'll start on the other side of the yard. You'll see Abigail had a good eye for color." He didn't let go of her hand.

"You said Gram's dream was to restore the house to its former glory," she said with studied casualness. "I think it looks good as it is."

"She was very passionate about it." He seemed surprised that she didn't know. "If she hadn't needed it as a place to live, I believe she might have turned it into a museum."

Catherine stared at him, astonished. How clueless had she been to Gram's dreams? It was beginning to dawn on her how much focus she'd put on her work. *Shame on me!*

"She felt the Stanhopes needed to be remembered for all they did in this community." His lip tipped upward. He stubbed his toe in the grass and seemed to be thinking about something that amused him.

"You probably already know this, but Abigail told me that when she and your grandfather 'courted,' her future father-in-law, Obadiah, would hide beside the porch and eavesdrop. He wanted to make sure she was the kind of girl who would be loyal to the Stanhope name. Once, apparently, he lost his balance and fell headfirst into the bushes. He came stumbling out of the shrubbery but he never lost his composure. Instead, he brushed the leaves off his coat and breezed by saying, 'Just passing through.' She loved that story."

"Gram adored being a Stanhope," Catherine said. "As a kid it sometimes felt like it set me too much apart from my friends. I was the little rich girl. I worked hard to dispel that notion." Maybe that was why Gram had been more enthusiastic about the Stanhope legend than she. It had been tough sometimes to feel so set apart in so many ways—an orphaned, wealthy little girl.

"Gram said it was exciting to be a part of history," she continued. "Funny, as a kid I never really understood what she meant. I suppose I do now, given all that my great-grandfather's generosity has done for this town and the region, but I've always been a little lukewarm about it compared to Gram. She had real zeal for it."

"I'd have it, too, if I were you. This is an amazing place, everything from the tray ceilings and Tiffany chandeliers to the gardens. What's not to love?"

There was a boyishness about him as he spoke of the house. Will's passion made his dark eyes sparkle. Catherine regretted her own lack of enthusiasm. He pulled a pocketknife out of his jeans, bent over a rose bush and carefully chose a luscious, perfectly shaped blossom. He cut it, ran the blade along the stem to take off the barbs and handed it to her.

"Of course, I grew up in a working-class family

and was one of those kids who always rode my bike by the big houses in wealthy neighborhoods dreaming that one of them would be mine one day."

"And what happened?" Catherine tucked the rose in her hair.

He threw back his head and laughed, a pleasant, musical sound that lifted her spirits. "Nothing much. Although I thought I was taking a road to fame and wealth, it turned out to be a dead end."

"As a gardener and caretaker?"

"No. Even as a kid I would have known that those professions didn't lead to wealth. After I graduated from college, I spent several years as a musician with a band, traveling from place to place—state fairs to barbecue joints— wherever we got a gig. I didn't come out of that a rich man."

"Was it fun?" Catherine asked wistfully. That seemed a rather exotic life compared to her own— college, law school, becoming a junior partner, being primed for even greater things in the firm, practicing law until she either went mad or died.

He looked at her, his eyes dancing. "It was phenomenal. Best years of my life in some ways—free, rowdy, playful—but then I grew up."

They walked back to the porch and she watched him settle into the chair cushions. He crossed one long leg over the knee of the other and settled back, looking as if he was born to be there.

"What did you do after you grew up?" She absently fingered a carrot stick.

"I still admired those beautiful homes, so I went into the construction business."

"So you were a contractor?"

"Yes. My partner and I own the business. I ran a lot of jobs and traveled from site to site. I even learned how to behave myself."

She looked at him, waiting for some more explanation but none was forthcoming.

"Then Abigail hired me to fix up her house and do the maintenance around this place. My sister was dying and I knew I had to settle down and make a home for my nephew. Plus, the place had gotten to be way too much for Abigail, but I'm sure you already knew that."

Gram had never complained. Catherine almost wished she would have. She'd offered a time or two to find help for her grandmother, but Abigail wouldn't hear of it. "It is good exercise, don't take that away from me," she'd always said.

"I'm here full-time until the house is done," Will continued. "It's a big job. Like I told you, it's going to take a couple years, at least, to complete it."

A couple of years! "What will you do now that Gram is gone?"

He looked at her oddly. "Same as before, I guess. She set up a fund for the house, from which I'm paid, and I have a contract for the work. Since part of my compensation is living in the guesthouse, I hope to continue. Even though she's gone, I know Abigail wanted Hope House restored. I made her a promise that I'd get it done no matter what.

"It's to my advantage, too," he said, more to himself than to her. "One less reason for my family to think that I'm not the best choice to raise my nephew."

"That's ridiculous!" Catherine practically shouted. "I've known you only a couple days and I'd already vouch for you!"

"You would?" His eyes gazed so intently into her that she squirmed.

"Let's just say that I support your effort and I'd be happy to tell your family what I've observed about you and Charley together." She couldn't commit to more and didn't want to go back on any promises, but she really did want to see Will and Charley together permanently. But the two of them living on Stanhope property complicated things greatly, she realized.

Gram should have talked to her about this. Of course, Gram had approached the subject of the house with her a couple times, but Catherine hadn't been interested, and had always allowed the conversation to drift to other things.

Now she was stuck with a permanent resident handyman living on her property and counting on making his home there. She had no place for him to go once she sold the house, which she had every intention of doing. She needed to move on and not look back. Surely Gram would have understood that.

Catherine was not necessarily proud of the woman she'd become—career-oriented, hard-driving, a little callous—since she'd been practicing law, but it had also taught her to be practical. Keeping this house was utterly impractical. Besides, she'd sold her home and quit her job to start her new life. She couldn't allow herself to be saddled down now.

The biggest problem she could see on the horizon—other than the devastating blow that losing Gram had already dealt—was how to tell Will Tanner that his job and his home would be disappearing as soon as she put this house on the market. She'd have to look at his contract, of course, to see exactly what Gram had promised him, hopefully no more than a month's notice on the guesthouse. It was obvious that Charley needed Will and vice versa. It would be tragic if something she did separated them…but she couldn't think about that. Right now, with the scent of roses wafting up at her, she could barely think at all.

Chapter Six

Charley shuffled around the corner of the house just as Catherine and Will were cleaning up after lunch. He moved as if he were suspended in molasses and his shoes scuffed roughly on the sidewalk. His arms were crossed, his eyes down and his lower lip protruding. It was a sad little picture, Catherine thought. The last child she'd seen looking that miserable had been a pawn in the nasty chess game called divorce.

"What's wrong, buddy?" Will opened his arms to the little boy and Charley crawled into the embrace. "You look pretty upset."

"Mikey told me that his mother said my mom was an all-co-hol-ick. Is that true, Uncle Will? Is that a bad thing to be?"

Catherine and Will's eyes met over the top of Charley's head. Some people were just too thoughtless for words.

Charley wiped away a tear. "My mom was *nice*. She couldn't be a bad thing, right?"

"Nice people can be alcoholics. Anyone can. She was a great mother, right?"

His head bobbed enthusiastically. "We played dominoes and picked flowers and took walks. She always said we were having homemade fun, which is the best kind. "

Catherine saw the anguish in Will's eyes.

"Do you know what, Charley? I absolutely agree with her." Catherine touched his baby-soft cheek. "It is the best kind. Gram and I baked cookies and drew pictures. Sometimes, when we were bored, we walked uptown and counted the lines in the sidewalk. We couldn't step on the lines, of course, only count them. That was our rule."

The sadness in the boy dissipated. Catherine was reminded of morning mist touched by the sun.

"Can we do it now?" Charley asked.

"Do what? Bake?"

"No, count lines in the sidewalk." He scrambled out of Will's arms. "Come on!"

"Buddy, I've got too much to do to…" Will protested.

"Not so much that you can't take a walk with us." Catherine jumped to her feet. "Gram and I always started right in front of the house."

Charley's eyes glittered with pleasure. With an amused sigh, Will followed them.

"We really don't have time for this, you know," Will said softly to Catherine as they walked slowly behind Charley. He happily jumped sidewalk cracks and counted aloud, obviously overjoyed with the attention of the adults.

"We don't have time not to," she responded, delighting in Charley's antics. The child brought out something maternal in her—an unaccustomed but pleasurable feeling.

"You're the boss," Will said, smiling.

Soon they approached Main Street. Pleasant had always prided itself on its quaint main thoroughfare. There was a wrought-iron bench with a shepherd's hook in front of each store, with baskets of petunias and pansies. Window boxes rioted with geraniums and hanging vines, and from each streetlight hung a small banner saying Welcome to Pleasant.

Charley flung himself onto the bench in front of Wilders' Drug and waited for the adults to catch up.

"Tired?" Catherine asked, joining him.

Will snorted. "He always gets tired right about here, no matter how much sleep he's had."

Catherine winked at the boy. "I always did, too. Gram said it was genetically impossible for me to pass by Wilders' without going in for an ice-cream cone. Want to get one?"

Charley was off the bench and inside the building before she could blink.

"Now you've started something," Will warned cheerfully. "You'd better keep a pocketful of change for every time you pass this store."

"Let's just not tell Charley what I did as a child. My grandmother always had a charge account here and I would buy ice cream and charge it to her. Sometimes twice a day."

"You're right. Keep that to yourself." Will opened the door for her and they entered the store that sold everything from drugs to magazines and ice cream to hair combs, nail polish, gardening gloves and toys.

They found Charley in the back, sitting on a fountain stool swinging his legs and talking to Mrs. Wilder as she dished up an enormous bubblegum ice-cream cone.

"Here you are." She greeted them with a smile that Catherine remembered from her childhood. "What kind of cone would you like?"

"None for me, I…" Will began.

"Peppermint for me, a double," Catherine interjected. "And Mr. Tanner will have the same." Charley gave her a thumbs-up.

As they strolled down Main Street finishing their cones, someone called out to them.

"Hey, Catherine! Will!"

Becky Barnard, a classmate and friend from high school, burst from her antiques store, Becky's Attic, onto the sidewalk. "I didn't get a chance to talk to you after the funeral. There were so many people around. I wanted to see you before you left town." Her round, sweet face grew somber. "I'm sorry about…"

"Thank you." Catherine said quickly, wanting to avoid the subject. "How are you?"

Will touched Catherine's arm. "I'll follow Charley. You visit with Becky. We'll walk back on the other side of the street and pick you up."

She nodded and waved them on before turning again to Becky. "So you're still running the antiques shop."

"You know me, I love the old stuff. I've also added gift items. If I can get people through the door to buy a birthday card or baby gift, maybe they'll stay and fall in love with an armoire or an old grandfather clock."

"So business is growing, then? I'm glad." In high school Becky had been the class history buff and she'd carried that interest in the past right into her current-day occupation. She had no doubt that Becky could rattle off the history and time period of every item in the shop.

"It's practically out of control these days," Becky admitted. "I do a lot more traveling for the shop than I ever used to. My mother and sisters come in to help me when they can, but I'm afraid I'm not going to be a one-woman operation much longer."

"I've always thought your business would be

interesting," Catherine admitted. "Hope House is filled with antiques."

"Beautiful ones, I might add."

"Would they be valuable?" Catherine asked curiously.

"I'd send an appraiser in to tell you something like that. My guess is that the contents of that house would be worth a small fortune."

Catherine wondered if Gram was turning over in the grave because her granddaughter had even broached such a question.

Becky, she realized, was eyeing her questioningly. "Emma says you're planning to be in Pleasant for a while. Is that true?"

"For a while," Catherine echoed, not willing to be pinned down to a date. "I recently resigned from my job in Minneapolis. I'd planned to come home and regroup before I move on. I'd counted on Gram being here...." She felt her throat tighten. "Now I don't know what I'll do with myself."

"Looks like you're entertaining yourself with the gorgeous Will Tanner. Every woman in town has drooled over him a time or two."

Catherine laughed. "He is a good-looking man, but I didn't pick him. I inherited him." She told Becky about Abigail hiring him to work on Hope House.

"I think you came out ahead. Will certainly improves the scenery."

Catherine smiled. She certainly couldn't argue with that.

"I know this is a crazy idea," Becky said hesitantly, "and you probably have your hands full, but…oh, never mind." She blushed. "It was a stupid idea."

"What?"

"I thought that if you wanted to get out of the house, you might want to come by and help me at the shop sometime, that's all." She waved a hand as if to dismiss the idea. "I shouldn't have even considered it. You must be up to your eyeballs in things you have to accomplish. It might be a little like the old days—you and me hanging out, laughing. And I'd have someone besides my mother to call on for help."

Catherine responded without thinking. "I'd love to!"

"You would? Why? I mean…I never…"

"I'm going to be at Hope House for an indefinite period of time. I'm not accustomed to being alone 24/7. It will be good for me to have an excuse to get away for a couple hours. Jerry Travers told me he could use occasional help, too, and I'm seriously thinking about it—back-room stuff, no court appearances. As long as you don't mind my somewhat erratic hours, why not?"

Becky's pretty round face beamed. "That would be awesome! Let me know when you are available. Frankly, I've gotten a little tired of being alone with the business. Just knowing you were coming around once in a while would do wonders for me." Then her features darkened. "I can't pay you much, of course. And you being a lawyer and all, I'm sure you're used to big money."

Catherine didn't say that being Gram's sole heir, she already had more than enough to last a lifetime. She knew Becky needed to feel she was employing her or she would think she was imposing upon her friend's time. "I work for minimum wage," Catherine informed her cheerfully, "and not a cent more."

Becky studied her for a long while before she threw her arms around Catherine. "Thank you so much. We'll be in touch."

As Becky retreated into her shop, Will and Charley appeared on the other side of the street. Charley was carrying a gigantic red, white and blue lollipop. "Look what Uncle Will bought me, Catherine! It's gi-normous."

"Aren't you lucky!" Catherine didn't try to suppress her smile. Will and Charley walked across the street, their resemblance to each other striking. Big and Little, that's what they were. Looking at Charley told Catherine exactly what Will had looked like as a child, and seeing Will told her about the man Charley would become.

"Did you have a nice visit?" Will asked when they reached her.

"I did." She eyed Charley. "Aren't you afraid he's going to have a sugar high?"

"Nah. He'll do what he always does—save most of it for later. One of those things can last him a week. Charley is the disciplined one in our family."

Catherine slipped her arm around the boy and pressed her cheek to the top of his head. He smelled like sunshine, shampoo and little boy.

They walked a while before Catherine said, "Becky asked me to work at her shop occasionally. I'll need something to do if I'm going to be in Pleasant for a while."

"I'm glad to hear you'll be staying a while."

She was startled by the genuineness in his voice. He really did sound glad.

"I suppose I'd better get back to the house," Will said reluctantly. "This is nice, but…"

"I've never seen anyone so eager to work as you are."

"Why am I so passionate about getting this done, you mean?" They strolled down the sidewalk toward Hope House. Charley lagged behind, licking on the lollipop. "I'm not much of a man if I can't finish what I start."

"That's what motivates you?"

"It's always been important to me, but now, as a father, I'm determined to carry through on my promises. Charley needs a role model. He heard me make promises to Abigail. I won't disappoint him either."

He was saying things Catherine didn't want to hear. "But Charley is young. He can't understand, and Abigail is gone. She would never know."

Will skewered her with his gaze. "But we're going to meet again. I'm counting on it."

That was exactly what her grandmother would have said. Was she the one who was misguided here? She'd always considered herself to be a lot like Abigail—but her grandmother had been plunging her roots even deeper into Pleasant while Catherine had been trying to tear hers up to free herself.

Oh, Gram, why did you die on me now? What were you thinking about this house and Will Tanner? What would you think about me?

Confusion ran rampant in her. Before she'd left the city, selling Hope House had seemed so logical, but here…

An overpowering loneliness engulfed her.

"Are you okay?" Will asked.

"Nothing that seeing Gram again wouldn't cure."

She ached at the sympathetic look he gave her. It said, as clearly as if he'd spoken aloud, that he understood.

"I was going to the lumberyard to pick up a few things. I promised Charley he could go, too, but we could hang around if you want me to."

His generosity made her feel even worse. He was selfless just when she felt so selfish. "No, go ahead. I'll be okay. Take Charley with you. I'll entertain myself here. It's not like there's nothing to do." The problem was that there was so much to do that she didn't know where to begin.

He pulled a scrap of paper and a stubby carpenter's pencil out of his pocket. "Here's my cell-phone number. Call me if you need me for anything."

"Okay. Now shoo."

She watched the two of them climb into the pickup and head out. What was Will's sister-in-law even thinking to consider separating them? With that thought rolling around in her head, she entered the house.

When they'd gone, Catherine closed the door and turned to lean against it. Without Will and Charley the house became a cavernous space with too-high ceilings and strange echoes. The massive chandelier loomed over a dining table that seated twenty with ease. The sideboards had as many cupboards as some kitchens. The place made her feel small and insignificant, just as she had as a child in this enormous room.

A scratching noise from the kitchen made her look up. Emma Lane popped into the dining room through a swinging door. Her arms were full of tablecloths.

"Hello, dear, I hope you don't mind. I washed

these after the gathering the other day and I wanted to put them away. The back door was open…."

"You're welcome here anytime, Emma. Gram viewed you as a sister."

"We were," Emma said soberly, "sisters in Christ. Oh, how I miss your grandmother." Then she seemed to pull herself out of the somber mood. "I see you've been spending time with Charley Tanner. Isn't he the cutest boy imaginable? And his uncle isn't bad either."

"Emma!"

The older woman smiled sagely. "I'm old, dear, not blind." Then, changing the subject, Emma asked. "What are your plans now, Catherine? What about Hope House?"

"My life is no longer in Pleasant," Catherine said frankly. "I have had several offers and one is more appealing than the rest. But Gram loved this house and it's such a part of her that…" Her voice trailed off.

"What do you see for yourself in the next few years?"

Catherine squeezed her eyes shut as if behind her lids a movie screen rolled with pictures of her life. Nothing there. She didn't want to go back to her old life and she'd never even considered living in Pleasant a viable option. It was too small, the kind of place that was good for married couples with children, not single women with high aspirations.

And the future? Strange, despite her plans to teach, the movie screen in her mind was a blank canvas, too.

"I'm thinking I should move somewhere and do something," she finally said weakly. "Whatever that means."

"If you just put it in God's hands, He'll work it out."

"Don't you think I should be involved in the decision-making process?"

Emma looked startled. "Oh, my dear, don't you know that when we try to direct God rather than allowing Him to guide us that we often mess it up? His plan might be one you don't like—until you get there."

After Emma had gone, the house seemed even emptier and her mind more confused.

Catherine did now what she had done so many times as a child. She mounted the stairs to the second floor. She refused to look at the construction mess Will had amassed in the hall and continued to the attic on the third floor of the house.

She opened the door and a warm, dusty smell assaulted her nostrils, the same familiar odor she recalled from her childhood. The sun's heat collected here on the top floor and the windows were opened no more than once or twice a year when Gram did a cursory sweeping of the floors. It felt warm, cloistering and inviting, just as it had when she was small.

Her steps were sure and familiar as she walked to the far corner, passing old trunks and cardboard boxes tied with twine and a graveyard of nonfunctioning vacuum cleaners and floor sweepers. There were the bookshelves she'd spent so much time studying. The Anne of Green Gables and Nancy Drew books her mother had owned were there, as was her own eclectic collection.

And there was the stack of suitcases that had held her captivated for so many hours of her childhood. She opened the top case. It was filled with costume jewelry. The Hope diamond could be lurking in there for all she knew. As a child she had worn string upon string of fake pearls and a floppy straw hat as she served tea to a tiny tableful of her favorite dolls and stuffed animals.

She opened a small cabinet and carefully withdrew a rusty-brown teddy bear with a missing ear and a faded red scarf around his neck. Mr. Bobkins Bear, her most precious childhood confidant. Tenderly, she cradled the bear in her arms, recalling the vivid memories surrounding him. He'd been all she had the day she'd come to live at Hope House, and for more than a year Catherine had never let it out of her sight.

She held the ragtag bear in front of her and demanded, "What should I do, Bobs? My life is suddenly a blank canvas and I don't like it." Only once before had everything been wiped away from her. Back then, Gram had taken her in, but Gram wasn't here anymore.

A sob caught in her throat and she sank to the floor, Bobkins against her cheek. She felt as lost and alone as she had the first time she'd arrived at Hope House.

Chapter Seven

It was late afternoon when Will found Catherine.

She'd fallen asleep curled on a thick rug in the attic, her head on a ragged bear. Dust motes drifted in the sunlight through the narrow, small-paned windows.

He wondered where she'd gone. He'd been making noise all afternoon, ripping up floorboards and nails that squealed in protest after being disturbed after all these years. It wasn't until Emma called to ask if she was still at Hope House that he'd grown concerned. The attic was the last place he'd looked and he wouldn't have checked there but for a nagging instinct and a little past experience.

There was a lot about Catherine's childhood that resembled Charley's. She, like Charley, would have found a hiding place to escape to until the world seemed like a safer place.

He was exactly right.

Cautiously, he moved closer, glad for the opportunity to study her freely. She was everything he'd imagined she would be and more. Although tall, Catherine was finely built with slender fingers and graceful arms and neck. There was a resilient cast to her sleeping features, he noted, and she slept with her lips barely parted, a strong woman with a tender side. Will felt drawn to her like iron shavings to a magnet.

Accidentally he bumped the toe of his boot against a claw-footed side table. On the table was an old mantel clock, its pendulum stilled for years. But when it was jarred, it managed a grating *bong* sound that made Catherine sit up, eyes wide. "What's happened?"

"I'm sorry. I didn't mean to wake you. Emma said you hadn't stopped at her place and I hadn't seen you…"

She looked intrigued. "So you came into the attic? How…"

The expression on her face was priceless. Puzzled, uncertain and pink from sleep. And she had a line running down one cheek made by the seam that ran down the teddy bear's back.

He sat on a discarded footstool so he was on her level.

"When Charley first came to live with me, more than once I discovered him in the eaves of the guesthouse where the broken wicker lawn furniture, dressers with splintered drawers and mismatched chairs from the big house were. Charley had set up a little fort in the jumble, with walls made of laddered chairs and the backs of dressers. He decorated it with pillows and blankets scavenged from the bedrooms. He kept his army of toy soldiers bivouacked there, and an album of photos of him and his mother."

"His hideaway," she murmured.

"Charley felt safe up there, so I never tried to talk him out. It was a small, hidden place Charley could call his own. Eventually, when he began to feel comfortable, he forgot his hideaway and came down to earth—literally."

"So you figured that one lost little soul might act like another?"

"I don't know about that. I just knew that if I were put in a new situation like yours or Charley's, I'd try to find a space of my own." He felt his throat tighten as he added, "I'd want somewhere to go when I wanted to think…or cry."

He knew his words had struck something in Catherine because her eyes filled with tears. "You do understand your nephew—and me." She pulled at the scarf on the teddy bear's neck and began to retie it as if to keep her hands busy.

"Charley is as lucky to have you as I was fortunate to have Gram. If I'd remained with my aunt and uncle, I would have had a very different

life—boarding school, probably, and nannies.
There's nothing wrong with that, but it was so much
better to grow up here, free to roam and play and
to have more love than I could even absorb."

Will thought back to the funeral when he'd met
Catherine's aunt Ellen for himself.

Ellen had looked as if she'd come off a magazine
cover with her perfect makeup, nails and clothes.
He tried to imagine a small child like Catherine
holding her hands out for a messy bear hug and
he couldn't do it. As fond as her aunt might be of
Catherine, it was no wonder Catherine was grateful
to Abigail for fighting for custody and not allowing them to sweep the little child she'd been away
into Ellen and Max's non-child-friendly life. From
what little conversation he'd had with Catherine's
relatives, he guessed that even her aunt and uncle
would say that now.

His gut tightened and again he felt the sick feeling, the troublesome concern, he'd been repressing.
He'd tried, with some success, not to think about it,
but Catherine's words made the worry wash over
him.

Catherine saw Will's expression change and his
body stiffen. What had she said that would make
him respond so viscerally to her comments? "Will,
what's wrong?"

He ran his fingers through his hair, stirring
up the natural waves that some women would no

doubt love to run their fingers through. Not her, of course.

It was a long while before he spoke. "You and Charley have a lot in common. I've told you before that his aunt and uncle—my brother, Matt, and sister-in-law, Sheila—don't like the fact that I have Charley. They want him to live with them. They think Charley needs both a male and a female influence in his life."

It did change things about Will's situation, she knew. Gram had had to take legal action to ensure that she would live with her. Ellen and Max had had money for lawyers, but Gram had had more.

Fortunately for Catherine's sake, they'd agreed to put the past behind them once the custody decision was made. To her aunt and uncle's credit, they had never held it against Gram for what she'd done. Eventually they'd come to appreciate the life she'd given their niece. But that result was the exception rather than the rule. People rarely came out of legal wrangles to form amicable relationships afterward.

"And your relationship with your brother and his wife is…" She left the questions hanging. It was none of her business, really, only her legal curiosity. "You don't have to answer that."

"It's a simple answer. My sister-in-law, Sheila, distrusts me and she'd do anything she could to take Charley away from me even though Charley's mother asked me to care for him."

"Did she put it in writing?" Catherine asked.

"No. So Sheila thinks my sister was ambivalent about my raising Charley. Sheila never even visited Annie while she was ill, yet she thinks she should be raising her son."

"Why does she distrust you?" Catherine sat cross-legged on the floor, her elbows resting on her knees. Something changed in his facial appearance when he talked about the child—the masculine features softened and his dark eyes lit as if he were smiling. She felt terribly drawn to him when he was like that. He adored that little boy and it showed in every fiber of his being. How could his sister-in-law miss that?

"We go back a long way, Sheila and I," he said.

"Something happened back then?"

"We were all in college at the same time. My brother, Matt, is a couple years younger than I am. When he started dating Sheila, he was obsessed with her. He seemed more like an animal being driven to slaughter than a man in love, however."

Will's expression grew pensive as he recalled the past. "Matt always liked to have fun. He was a real party guy in his day, but he is also pretty passive by nature.

"He didn't have a chance once Sheila decided to marry him. Not only is she a stunner, a blonde with incredible blue eyes, but she's intelligent and can be very witty. Matt admires that in a woman. He didn't seem to notice that Sheila kept him on a short rope or that when she said 'Jump,' he said 'How high?'" Will commented bluntly.

His eyes flashed angrily. "She also had the verbal skills to twist facts to suit her needs. Apparently Matt has far more tolerance for lying than I do. Fabrications, distortions, I find them all unacceptable. As far as I can tell, he didn't really see the rest of her, at least not the less admirable traits."

Will shifted uneasily, as if even the thought of his sister-in-law made him uncomfortable. "Her personality is as frosty as her eyes. I've learned never to underestimate Sheila. She'll do just about anything to get her own way. I've watched her manipulate my brother enough years to know that. Maybe if they'd have had kids of their own…"

"Anything? Surely not…"

"You don't know Sheila." He grimaced. "Unfortunately you might get to know her one of these days. She'll probably stop by to check up on us."

Catherine looked stricken.

Was that a good sign, Will wondered, or a bad one? There was only one way to find out. "I was wondering if you could help…"

At that moment Charley clattered up the stairs. He stepped gingerly into the room, wide-eyed with wonder, and looked around the fascinating jumble of boxes, furniture and lamps. "It's magic up here!"

Through the eyes of a child, it just might be, Will thought. After all, he'd just found a princess sleeping on a teddy bear. What could be more magical than that?

"I have to get something for Charley to eat for dinner. Want to join us?" he asked.

"I don't want to be a bother...."

"No trouble. By the look of you, you can't eat much. It will be like adding a bird to the guest list. Give me a half hour and I'll think of something. Then come over."

Catherine was grateful. No wonder Gram had liked having him around.

After Will disappeared, she took a shower in the small downstairs bath, blew her hair dry and scavenged her old closet for something to wear. Other than some plaster dust, the black sundress she found was perfectly adequate. She'd forgotten about it until now, but still liked the lacy cutouts in the fabric in the back of the dress from shoulder to waist.

Catherine realized that she was tempted to dress nicely for the handyman, something she hadn't done for anyone in a long time. Of course, she hadn't dated much recently. There'd been little time for a life outside the law firm. It wasn't just Will who made her wish for a little blush and mascara. She simply wanted to feel like a woman again.

After she was done, she decided to sit on the front porch for a few minutes. It was cool and shady there, and it soothed her to rock back and forth in Gram's white rocker. She was reminded again, however, that sitting on one's porch in Pleasant was far more social than lazing on one's deck on a condo in the city.

"Evening, Ms. Catherine." It was Stanley of Stanley's Meat Market. He trotted up the steps and thrust out something wrapped in white locker paper. "Smoked bacon. A little welcome-back-to-Pleasant gift."

"Thank you, Stanley, you shouldn't have." She took the package eagerly. Stanley sold the best bacon in three counties.

"'Course I should have. You're one of us, Ms. Catherine, and now you're back. We're glad to have you." With that, he tipped an invisible hat and turned to stride down the steps.

Catherine stared at his retreating back as he moved down the sidewalk. One of us? She hadn't thought of herself as a part of Pleasant that way in many years. But here was a pound of bacon to prove that someone felt she still was.

At the appointed time she strolled across the carpetlike lawn to Will's, wondering what, if anything,

Gram and Tanner had done there. The last time she remembered being in the guesthouse, it had been a catchall for unwanted furniture and gardening equipment.

She rapped on the rim of the screen door. Will waved her in with a dish towel in his hand. Catherine entered and cast her gaze about the room. The little apartment was transformed and Will's masculine touch was everywhere.

The walls, which had once been painted an optimistic but ugly yellow, were now terra-cotta red and fawn. The clip-on shades on the overhead lights had been replaced with pendant lighting and a small chandelier made of antlers. There was log furniture with fabric-covered pillows in dramatic southwestern designs. On the walls were prints of running horses, trumpeting elk and Charley. There had to be a dozen black-and-white photos of the child. In some of the poses was a lovely but worn-looking woman who was obviously Will's sister, Annie.

"It's awesome in here!" she finally managed. "Like a hunting lodge."

"That's the look I was going for," Will said as he lifted a sheet of salmon steaks from the oven and with a spatula placed them over mounds of couscous. "How do you like the furniture? I made it myself."

As if Will had just rung a dinner bell, Charley

appeared in the doorway. He, too, had showered and his hair stuck up in damp spikes all over his head.

"You forgot to comb your hair, buddy."

Charley made a face and disappeared. When he returned, his hair was slicked against his forehead. He slid into his place at the table and folded his hands. "Can I pray?"

"You bet. Give it your best shot, buddy," Will said.

Catherine watched and listened in amazement as the child began to pray.

"Dear God, thanks for fish, especially salmon the way Uncle Will cooks it, and for cabbage even though it's gross, and for coos-coos." He sounded like a little dove as he said it. "And thank You for Jesus and my mom and my uncle and for Ms. Catherine, who's come to help us fix up Hope House. And take care of Gram. You're lucky you've got her now. Amen."

Catherine didn't even realize there were tears streaming down her face until Will swiped his finger across her cheek.

"He affects me that way, too, sometimes," Will said so softly that Charley, who was digging into his meal, didn't hear.

Things were getting out of hand. Everything Charley and Will did seemed to touch Catherine at her core. She looked down to spread her napkin in her lap. She didn't want Will to see her expression. She was a hairbreadth away from falling for these two charmers, and what a complication that would be.

After dinner Will excused himself to read to Charley and hear his prayers while Catherine washed up in the kitchen. When he returned, she was sitting on the couch, her feet curled beneath her and her eyes on a thick tome about the restoration of old houses. When she'd opened the cover she'd read the inscription there:

To Will Tanner, who's going to help me fulfill my dreams—be sure to keep a hammer in your hand and God in your heart! Abigail Stanhope

"Your grandmother gave that to me," he said as he sat down on the far end of the sofa.

"So I see." Things were fast becoming more difficult than she'd anticipated. Along with Hope House, Catherine hadn't counted on being heir to two men who knew exactly how to get to her heart, even if they didn't realize it yet.

Chapter Eight

At the end of the evening Catherine found herself oddly reluctant to leave the cozy home Will and Charley had created for themselves. It defined the word *sanctuary*. She felt sheltered and protected there, something she'd only experience with Gram until now. To guard herself from the pain of losing the people she loved, she'd toughened herself so much that she had never really let anyone see her be vulnerable. That had felt dangerous until now... until Will.

"What's on the agenda for tomorrow?" she asked, forcing herself to sound perky and enthusiastic. "Putting the bathroom floor back together, I hope."

"I'm thinking of taking off the storm windows and putting up the screens before it gets any warmer outside."

Catherine began to realize she'd been an oblivious

teenager, unaware of all the maintenance for Hope House that Gram had quietly taken care of while Catherine was off with her friends.

"In the spring the glass storm windows have to be taken off, washed and put away. The screened versions, which are stored in the stalls of the carriage house, are replaced so the inside windows can be opened in the summer to get a breeze. Then in the fall…"

"You start all over again. Couldn't you just change out the windows for something more modern?"

He looked at her askance. "It wouldn't be authentic and historical. Abigail would have none of it."

Again, it had taken Will to remind her of her own grandmother's wish and dreams. She wasn't sure if she resented it or if she simply envied Will for the relationship he and Gram had shared.

"May I walk you home?" Will asked.

"Emma's place isn't far," Catherine halfheartedly protested. He was gentlemanly, too.

"Charley, it's time to get into bed. I'll be right back."

The little boy slid off his chair and walked to Catherine. He threw his arms around her and planted a wet kiss on her cheek before trucking off to the bedroom. "G'night, Ms. Catherine," he called over his shoulder.

"This really isn't necessary," Catherine protested as they walked outside.

"Of course it is. How is Charley ever going to know how to treat a lady if I don't teach him?"

"You're the perfect father, you know that?"

She heard him take a sharp breath. "I want to be. He sure deserves it. My sister and I were very close. I want to give him everything I couldn't give her."

Again Catherine found herself unable to speak. They walked in silence toward Emma's, but in her mind, she was petitioning for help.

Okay, Lord, I get it. This man and his little boy are something special, but I don't know what I can do about it. I won't be here all that long. I pray that You will send someone into their lives to help them. Please show Charley's aunt and uncle that Will is the best father for him. Bless this pair and keep close watch on them. Amen.

She paused at Emma's front door. "I'm going to have to stay in Gram's house soon." She laughed a little in the darkness. "Of course, someone tore up my bedroom, but I'm sure I can find another."

"Fortunately there are plenty to choose from. I'll move your things into any room you'd like in the morning."

Catherine considered her next words carefully. "I can't understand why some woman hasn't snapped you up, Will. Emma has been singing your praises. According to her, you've got it all—chivalry, compassion and cooking skills."

He laughed out loud. "Thanks for the kind words, but obviously you don't know me very well—I'm far from perfect." He leaned against the doorjamb, crossed his arms and studied her in the dim glow of a small porch light. "How about you? You're single, too. And smart. And beautiful."

She ignored the last part. "I've dated some, but for the most part I was married—to my work. If someone asked me out on a Saturday night but I had a legal brief to write, I always chose to go to the office. I've never felt I had the time it takes to build a relationship." She cleared her throat. "Or maybe I've just never met anyone I truly wanted to build a relationship with."

"I'm sorry." Will sounded genuinely sympathetic.

"It's okay. Gram always said that being happily single is far better than being unhappily married. I took her words to heart."

She sighed. "I've felt so sad and disoriented these past weeks—quitting my job, selling my home, leaving the city and losing Gram. It's as if I've been going through a series of nasty divorces."

"We're a fine pair," Will commented. "Independent, skittish…"

Catherine yawned. "Sleepy."

He laughed and without any self-consciousness, reached out and brushed a lock of hair from her eyes. His fingers were warm and gentle. "Good night, Catherine. Sleep tight. Don't let the bedbugs bite."

That was exactly what Gram had said to her every night since Catherine's arrival at Hope House. That silly phrase brought back a flood of warm memories, precious memories, something to cuddle up with. Will had an instinctive ability to touch her heart, she realized, and she liked it. In fact she liked everything about the man. *Everything*. She knew she would sleep like a log tonight.

The next morning, while Charley was still asleep, Will quietly put the coffee on to brew and sat with his Bible, enjoying some quiet reflection. The sweet solitude didn't last. His phone rang and Will ran to grab it before it woke Charley.

"Hello?"

On the other end he heard an edgy, impatient voice. "Good. You're home. Matt and I are driving up there today. We should arrive about noon. I don't suppose there's a decent restaurant in town, is there?"

"Morning, Sheila," Will said wearily. His sister-in-law always made him tired. Today was no exception.

"Well, is there?"

"You could come to my place."

"Neither your brother nor I eat frozen pizza," she said with a hint of disapproval in her voice.

"Don't worry. I'll scrape something together that will satisfy you. To what do I owe the honor of this visit?"

"You know. We don't want Charley camping out in a shack you've found when he can be here with Matt and me, in a real home."

Not in a million years would Will describe his brother's place as a real home. A home had to have heart. Instead, theirs had contemporary furniture that was all angles and drama, like Sheila herself. But once Sheila made up her mind, nothing would dissuade her. He gave her the address of Hope House and hung up.

With a groan, he leaned his elbows on the table. What a perfect way to ruin a beautiful morning.

A knock on the door interrupted his thoughts.

Catherine stood on his doorstep with one of Emma's coffee cakes in her hands. She took one look at his face and said, "Maybe this will cheer you up."

"I need all the help I can get." He took the plate from her hands and ushered her inside. "I just got a call from my sister-in-law. They're coming today to discuss Charley. There's nothing to talk about as far as I'm concerned, but stopping Sheila from coming is impossible now." He told her about their conversation about finding somewhere to eat.

"Why don't you have lunch at Hope House?"

Catherine asked. "There's plenty of space to visit. You can eat in the dining room."

"Where's the food going to come from? Sheila's already said she won't eat pizza."

"That's easy. I'll cook and serve. You won't have to leave Charley alone with them."

"Which is probably a good idea," Will admitted, "but I can't ask that of you."

"Sure you can. I saw you working long into the night to repair the damage I did to that wall. I owe you one. I'm also a very good cook. My grandmother taught me."

Will smiled a little at that. "Gee, how can I resist?"

"Great." Catherine was eager to get into Gram's kitchen. "You'll have to tell me what your sister-in-law likes to eat."

Will almost responded, "Nails and small children," but he resisted the impulse. That was unfair. Even though he had few fond feelings for his sister-in-law, he knew she'd try to be good to Charley. Will knew what she really wanted was his own head on a platter.

Despite even these dismal thoughts, Will felt a smile spread across his features. Catherine had surprised him. She'd proposed something he viewed as surprisingly intimate. She'd offered to share her home and cook for his family. A place warmed inside him, somewhere that until now only Charley could reach. It was a place that, since Annie had died, had been lonely and inaccessible—his heart.

Chapter Nine

Catherine already disliked Will's sister-in-law and they hadn't even met. He was obviously a wonderful father to Charley and loved the boy deeply. Why would someone doubt Will's ability to raise him?

To keep her mind busy, she worked on the lunch menu. She didn't want Sheila to be able to accuse Will of not feeding Charley the proper foods. Catherine headed for the kitchen to begin searching through Gram's cookbooks.

At eleven, just after she checked the lasagna she'd put in the oven, Will wandered into the kitchen. He looked grim.

"What's wrong?" she asked.

He scowled. "I'm getting my game face on to meet Sheila. How am I doing?"

"I'm shaking in my boots," she said lightly. "Now go get cleaned up. I've made lasagna, salad and iced tea. At eleven-thirty I'll bake the rhubarb crisp. That way it will still be warm when I serve it. All I have left to do is to set the table." She allowed some of her impishness to show in her smile. "How many forks and spoons does Charley know how to use? Can we impress Sheila with his table manners?"

Will burst out laughing. "You're really getting into this, aren't you?"

"Charley belongs with you. He loves you. I want to do my part to make sure that happens."

"You have no idea how much I appreciate this. Catherine, I…" He paused as if to pull himself together. "Charley knows how to use every fork and spoon you can throw at him, even the oyster fork and dessert spoon. It was a game he and Abigail played. She said that someday that bit of knowledge would come in handy."

"Well, today's the day."

"I'll be back shortly. I need to clean Charley up, as well." He shook his head as if he couldn't quite believe what he'd just said. "I'm acting like there's a social worker coming to determine if I'm a fit parent."

"In a way, there is," Catherine said softly, her heart heavy. "I'm sorry you have to go through this." Will smiled, shrugged, then walked out.

The doorbell rang forty-five minutes before the lasagna was done baking. They were early.

Not too early for Charley, however. Scrubbed and polished, the boy sat in one of the wing chairs with a book about birds in his lap. Will, exceedingly handsome in khakis and a button-down blue shirt, paced in front of the fireplace. Catherine wore one of Abigail's aprons and was ready to serve. It was fun to play house, but she hadn't expected the guests to be so early.

Will went to the door and opened it. A well-dressed couple that reminded Catherine a good deal of her own aunt and uncle stood on the other side. The woman breezed in and her husband trailed behind her, bobbing in her wake.

Sheila Tanner was a silvery blonde with short hair that was slightly spiked on top but tapered closely to her head and neck. Her silver earrings were expensive, and her makeup was flawlessly applied. Catherine admired the Gucci suit Sheila wore, but couldn't imagine how she'd react if a little boy with sticky hands and a dirty face ran up to her for a hug.

Matt's build was similar to Will's, as were the chiseled features and dark hair. Looking at Matt, however, was like looking through a scrim on a stage. He had a slightly stooped posture, unexpressive eyes and a defeated air. How brothers could look so much alike and yet be so entirely different was startling.

Catherine moved forward to greet the guests as Will seemed to be struck momentarily speechless. "Welcome to Hope House! Please come in."

That woke Will to his task. "Yes, please. Hello, Sheila, Matt."

Matt thrust out a hand to shake first Catherine's and then Will's. When he smiled Catherine saw something of Will there and Charley, as well.

Sheila brushed past Catherine as if she weren't even there, her eyes busy taking in the rich carved woodwork, the original art and the hand-tied rugs. "Why are we meeting here?" she asked. "I thought we were to meet at your place."

"This is his place," Catherine interjected sweetly. "Will has lived and worked on Hope House's premises for some time." *And you'd know that if you'd ever cared enough to visit your little nephew.*

Sheila spun toward Catherine. "And just who are you?"

"My name is Catherine Stanhope and I'm helping Will out today. We've got a few minutes before lunch. Would you like to take a stroll around town while we're waiting? You could get a feel for the place."

For the first time the pair glanced beyond the foyer to notice the little boy in the vast chair. Charley scrambled out and laid the thick book on the seat. His cowlick had escaped the hold of the gel Will had used, but he still looked like the scrubbed, immaculately dressed eight-year-old child of a Ralph Lauren magazine advertisement.

Charley, completely at ease in Hope House,

strolled across the room. With a comfortable man-of-the-house air, he stuck out his hand and said, "Hello, Aunt Sheila, Uncle Matt. It's nice to see you." His eyes danced with excitement. "I could show you my school and where I go to church if you want."

Unexpectedly, the brittle Sheila bent down on one knee to Charley's level. She reached out a manicured finger and gently touched his cheek. "Is it a long walk?" she asked.

"No. Come on!" Charley tugged on his aunt's hand. Then he glanced up at Catherine. "Are you coming with us?"

"I can go a few blocks, I suppose. We're waiting for the main course to finish cooking." She had a difficult time saying no to the little boy. Besides, Will's expression told her that he wanted her to come along.

Charley led the way, dancing ahead of Matt and Sheila, turning around occasionally to point out an important sight. "That's where there's a robin's nest every year and there are moles in the park and they don't have eyes. Not good ones, at least. And that's where my friend Mikey lives and here's…oh, hi, Mrs. Monroe." Charley eyes were big when he turned back to the group behind him. "This is my teacher!"

Mrs. Monroe bent to give Charley a hug. "I've missed you since school's been out!"

"I'll come and visit you," Charley assured her. He pointed at Will. "Just tell my dad where you live."

Catherine noticed Matt and Sheila exchange glances. They, too, had picked up on the fact that Charley had called Will "dad." They looked as if they were sucking sour lemons.

Mrs. Monroe smiled at Will. "I'm behind the meat market in the red house with white shutters. Do you know it?"

"Sure do."

"Please let him come sometime. Charley is such a delightful child. Everyone in school is crazy about him, from the kids to the janitor. I've loved having him in my class this year. He's so well behaved, too."

After Mrs. Monroe had gone, they continued to walk. Charley's chest had puffed out a bit at the compliment and he was strutting like a little peacock.

Catherine glanced at the time on her cell phone. "I've got to go back and take the lasagna out so it can rest. Please finish your stroll. Lunch will be ready when you get back." She put her hand on Will's forearm. "Good luck," she whispered.

"Thanks. See you in ten minutes." His expression told her ten minutes could feel like a lifetime with these people.

Catherine hurried away, knowing Will's gaze followed her.

When they returned to the house, Charley sauntered into the dining room, sniffed the air and said, "It smells great, Ms. Catherine. I'm starved!"

Catherine read the confusion on Matt and Sheila's faces. Obviously this was not how they'd expected this visit to play out.

Once Will had seated their guests, Catherine began to serve the meal. "Organic wild greens," she explained as she set the salads on the table. "The raspberry vinaigrette is homemade. I'll bring the veggie lasagna out in a few minutes. I hope you all like eggplant."

"Yum," Charley said enthusiastically. Will had told her the little boy had an unbridled enthusiasm for that vegetable. Perfectly comfortable with the mass of silverware Catherine had put out, he picked up his salad fork.

When Will cleared his throat, Charley paused.

"Would you like to say grace, buddy?"

"Sure." Praying came as naturally to Charley as breathing—a legacy left to him by his dying mother.

"Dear God, thanks for this food, especially for the dessert Ms. Catherine's got in the kitchen. And thanks for my uncle Will and…" he hesitated slightly "…for our company. Thanks for taking care of us. And bless Ms. Catherine and Abigail and my Sunday school teacher and my mom in heaven…"

Will cleared his throat again. Charley got the hint and added a hurried, "Amen."

When Catherine brought in the lasagna, she noted that Will looked as if he was being threatened with a Taser. Matt said little, deferring to his wife, who peppered Charley with questions about everything from his teacher and friends to math questions.

Quietly, Catherine disappeared into the kitchen and didn't return until she served the rhubarb crunch with vanilla ice cream. There hadn't been any raised voices over lunch, which likely meant that they were saving the bulk of the conversation for when Charley was out of the room.

"Oh, I couldn't," Sheila said as she looked at the dessert. She brushed her hand over her flat stomach.

Catherine laughed. "I feel that way, too, but not about this. Rhubarb isn't in season very long and I refuse to miss a spoonful of it. Just try it. Don't feel obligated to eat the whole thing." She was pleased that Sheila allowed her put the plate down in front of her.

"Will you join us, Catherine?" She heard a plea in Will's voice.

"I'd love to. Let me get my own dessert."

When Catherine returned to the table, Sheila and Matt studied her curiously. After they'd eaten in silence for a few moments, Sheila inquired, "You must be a good friend of Will to do this. Do you work here all the time?"

Catherine gave her a brilliant smile. "Not always, but I've been working very hard here this week."

"What is your position, exactly?" Sheila's tone intimated that she suspected some dark liaison between Will and Catherine.

Catherine laid down her fork and leaned forward, holding Sheila's gaze with her own. "Didn't Will tell you? I'm the *owner* of Hope House."

Will wanted to plant a kiss on Catherine's lips. Unchristian as it must be, he had to admit he enjoyed Sheila's snobbishness backfiring on her for once.

"Owner?" Sheila stuttered.

"Yes. Will is restoring Hope House. He was my grandmother's right-hand man and now he's mine. I simply don't know how we Stanhopes would function without him. If he ever needed a personal recommendation, I'd give him a glowing one, that's for sure."

Catherine's tone was so sincere that Will had to believe she was telling the truth and gratitude swelled inside him. It couldn't hurt his case with Sheila either.

Charley's small voice filled the stunned gap in the conversation. "Uncle Will, can I go upstairs to the attic and get my teddy bear? I left him there last night. And then can I go play with my friends?"

"Stay in the yard. I'm sure your aunt and uncle will want to see you again before they leave."

Charley nodded and bounded for the stairs as happy to be released as if he'd been sitting in an electric chair rather than a Chippendale. Moments later, they heard him clattering down the back staircase and into the yard.

"I should probably start clearing up," Catherine said and started to rise.

Will grasped her hand. "Please stay. There's nothing we're going to say that you can't hear."

He needed a friendly ally. He'd expected that Abigail would be the one cheering him on, not her granddaughter. But right now he'd take help wherever he could find it. He saw the surprise in Catherine's eyes but was relieved when she settled back into the chair.

"If you insist."

"Are you sure?" Sheila interjected. "We have to talk about private family matters, Will."

"It's okay. I considered Catherine's grandmother one of my best friends. I want her here."

He felt Catherine shift a little in her chair.

Was she uncomfortable? Right now Will didn't care. He wanted someone by his side who knew how much he cared about Charley. Catherine had seen them together. That would have to be enough.

Sheila wasted no time. "We have to discuss Charley."

"What's to discuss? You've seen him. He's a happy, healthy little boy. He's adjusted beautifully to living here with me."

"But he doesn't have two parents like a child deserves." Sheila looked to her husband for confirmation, but Matt sat stoically, staring straight ahead, arms across his chest.

His brother's body language couldn't have been much louder, Will thought. Matt didn't want to be here. Nor, if Will's hunch was correct, did he want to support Sheila in her quest for guardianship of Charley. But Matt had been Sheila's puppet so long that he was hardly going to stop now.

"Two parents don't guarantee happiness," Will pointed out, "any more than having only one parent means disaster. God designed us to have both a mother and a father, but I also know He can equip one parent to fill the bill if need be. Charley had a mother, and I keep that memory alive in him. Annie loved him with all her heart, and by the end, she really did know how to parent."

"She was a worthless alcoholic, Will, and you know it. Her priorities weren't all for Charley."

Will knew she was baiting him. Sheila wanted him to lose his temper so she would have another weapon in her arsenal against him.

"Annie was far from worthless." He frowned at his brother. "You know that, Matt, even though you never spent more than a half hour at a time with our sister in the final months of her life." He studied his brother. "How many times did you visit Annie? Twice? Three times?"

Matt's face contorted and he reddened. "I know what you're getting at, Will. No, I didn't spend enough time with Annie, but I did the best I could under the circumstances." Matt's gaze darted toward Sheila's face and away again as if he were seeking her confirmation for his words.

"Under the circumstances? You were on a trip in Europe most of the time she was dying!"

"Give me a break, bro. Those tickets cost thousands."

"And your sister's life was cheap? Is that what you're saying?"

"Don't twist his words," Sheila said sharply.

"Let my brother speak for himself for a change, Sheila."

They sat glaring at each other, daggers in their eyes.

This is going well, Will thought ruefully. Even when he was determined to keep the peace with Sheila, it backfired. When was his brother going to wake up and see this woman for who and what she really was? Or maybe he already knew but still continued to play along.

"Be realistic, Will," Sheila said. "We can give Charley everything he needs—top-notch schooling, friends with influential parents, opportunities in sports and music. When he's done with high school, he can go to any college he wants. Charley can be something."

"He's something already, Sheila. He's a happy little boy. He doesn't need a schedule to take him to the top in business or in society. He needs love and a chance to be a child without worries or cares. That's what I'm giving him."

"Growing up in a miniscule spot in the road with an uncle who, for some unknown reason, chose to leave a lucrative business to come to Hicksville to do what he pleased? You're a rebel, Will. Frankly, I don't want my nephew exposed to your random ways. He lived an unstructured life with his mother and now with you. The boy needs order in his life!"

Will had almost forgotten that Catherine was present until she said mildly, "I grew up here and I turned out okay, if that's what you're worried about."

"You?" Sheila, her claws still out, spat. "I'm not satisfied with just 'okay' for Charley."

Matt, who seemed to have been in a trance, finally spoke. "What do you do, Ms. Stanhope?"

"For the past several years I've been an attorney at the firm of Conrad, Connor & Cassidy in Minneapolis. Have you heard of them?"

Will was pleased to see both Sheila's and Matt's eyes widen.

"Yes, of course, it's a well-known firm," Matt said. "My company has had some dealings with them."

"Did they represent you?" The look on Catherine's face was sheer innocence.

Then Will noticed the predatory expression in Catherine's eyes. Instinctively he knew that she'd seen blood in the water and had begun to circle.

"No. They represented our opponents."

"I see. And did you win your case?" Catherine's tone was perfectly even and pleasant, but her eyes were still steely.

"No." Matt looked miserable and Sheila frustrated.

"I see. Don't feel too badly. It happens a lot when people come up against us." She rose from her seat. "I see you're out of coffee. I'll get some more." She headed for the kitchen and turned back at the door. "By the way, Mr. Conrad, Mr. Connor and Mr. Cassidy all grew up in small towns, just like I did."

Again, Will had the urge to take her into his arms and kiss her, knowing for sure that if he had a beautiful woman like her in his life, he'd keep her as close to himself as his own skin. The thought made him smile.

Chapter Ten

Sheila Tanner was a cool cookie, Catherine thought as she scrubbed the lasagna pan. Almost as calculating as the mother in that last disastrous case of hers. They could have been twins, both manipulating women who were after a child for all the wrong reasons. Catherine didn't doubt that Sheila loved Charley in her own way, but it was a little like the way of a turtle that lays its eggs and leaves. It was a penguin like Will who dedicated himself to parenthood.

To her surprise, Sheila suddenly walked into the kitchen.

"Thank you, the meal was wonderful."

"You're most welcome." Catherine's guard was up.

"He's a nice little boy, isn't he?" Sheila asked as she ran a finger along the counter. "Do you have children, Ms. Stanhope? Matt and I have never been able to have any of our own." She sounded almost wistful.

Catherine was surprised at Sheila's openness. "No. I've never been married."

"So you can see, then," Sheila said with a note of desperation in her voice, "why it's so important that Charley come to live with us."

"No, I really don't. Just because Will is single, that doesn't mean that he hasn't created a wonderful home for your nephew," Catherine pointed out. "He's a good man."

"But Charley needs a woman in his life!"

Catherine felt a wash of sympathy for the woman. Perhaps this was less about Will than about Sheila herself. "Or is it that you need a child in yours?" she asked gently, attempting to speak the truth without devastating the hearer. "I understand how precious having a child can be—but not at the expense of others."

Sheila blanched but didn't refute what Catherine had said. She was silent, lost in her own thoughts.

As Catherine cleaned the kitchen, she could hear Will saying goodbye to his guests.

Soon he appeared in the doorway looking haggard, as if he'd just tussled with a tigress. He walked in and took a stool on the far side of the counter. "What'd you think?"

"I think you've got your work cut out for you.

Sheila is what my colleagues at the law firm call a formidable opponent."

"That's what I'm afraid of. When Sheila wants something, she goes after it until she gets it. My brother is a prime example."

"Why doesn't he ever speak up? He's so much like you in looks, but in personality…"

"Matt's always been quieter than me, but now—especially since Annie died—he's practically mute. He's not happy. It's crazy to say, but he acts guilty. He doesn't look me in the eye. All I know is that Sheila's got a hold on him."

"Curious." Catherine folded the dish towel and hung it over the door handle on the stove. "And what did she mean when she called you a rebel who left a perfectly good business to come to Pleasant?"

"I have my own construction company. My partner currently runs it."

"And now you're my grandmother's handyman?" Her eyebrows lifted in surprise.

"I decided to take time off to make sure Charley had the attention he needed and Pleasant seemed the ideal place to do it. I'd been through here when I visited my cousin and always liked it."

He gave her a quirky, lopsided grin that did something odd to the pit of her stomach. "I'm *your* handyman now, Ms. Catherine. What do you say we get to work?"

* * *

The next morning Catherine awoke to a beam of early-morning light streaming into her room. She groaned and rolled over to look at the clock. It was earlier than she'd hoped to wake up. She was sure that all the work of the past week would have allowed her to sleep in, but she felt completely refreshed. There was no use wasting a perfectly good morning. She winced when her feet hit the floor, but the day lay ahead of her. She might as well get started.

After dressing quickly, she washed her face, brushed her teeth and pulled her long, thick hair into a ponytail. After grabbing a couple of granola bars from a jar on the kitchen counter, Catherine escaped Emma's house and headed down the street.

She didn't feel like going into the house to sort Gram's things. She still felt too raw for that. Instead, she would walk downtown and drop in at Becky's antiques shop.

Becky was delighted to see her. Catherine followed Becky to the center of the shop, which was cleverly arranged in vignettes. There was an inviting parlor with a petite rocker and footstool, a side table adorned with a knitting basket and a charming nursery room with a delicate white iron crib and old linens.

"Your timing is perfect," Becky said. "I've got the

electric kettle on. You'll have to try this new brand of raspberry tea I found. I'm considering setting up a little tea shop at the back of the store. Groups of ladies can shop and then have an English tea while they rest and regroup. While they do, I can wrap gifts with special paper and ribbon and play my harp. What do you think?"

Becky had taken harp lessons after graduating high school. Now she played for weddings and the occasional dinner parties. Even as a teenager, Becky had been a throwback to an earlier time, collecting porcelain dolls and silver brush-and-comb sets.

"I think it's absolutely marvelous!" Catherine said. "I hope you'll do plenty of advertising. It could mean great business for your shop."

Becky threw an arm over Catherine's shoulders. "See? You're helping me already. It's nice to have someone to talk things over with. My husband is a truck mechanic and every time I start talking about tea parties, hat pins or old sterling, his face goes blank. He'd do anything for me, mind you, but don't ask him if ladies prefer cream puffs or scones."

Becky took a vintage linen tablecloth off an inlaid desk, shook it out and spread it over a small table and then disappeared for a moment. When she returned, she was carrying two fragile cups and saucers. One bore the design of a delicate rose, the other that of twining ivy. She vanished again and this time returned with a teapot and a plate of shortbread. "There," she said with satisfaction as she set her burden on the table. "Now we can talk like ladies did before texting, Twitter and over-booked schedules interfered. I love the olden days. You will help me fold the flyers I have going out in a mailing tomorrow, won't you?"

An enormous orange-and-white cat waddled by, its pendulous stomach nearly touching the floor. It moved toward a throw rug in the nursery vignette and tipped itself onto its side.

"That's Genevieve," Becky said. "She's 'with kitten.' I expect her to give birth any second. Let me know if you want a kitten at Hope House. It will be a great mouser if its mother is any indication."

"I'll remember that," Catherine said.

They were quiet for a few moments before Catherine asked, "Do you ever tire of what you do?"

"Not for a minute. I'm happy to get up every morning so I can come here." Becky studied Catherine. "I take it you didn't feel quite the same way about your job."

Catherine almost laughed. The past few months it had taken everything in her power to gather the energy to go to the office. In comparison, folding flyers was a treat.

"You have fun every day," Catherine said. "This must be a little like playing house."

"It is. It's a joy for me to come to work."

"I can't remember the last time I had joy at work."

"No kidding? That's awful!"

"People who walk through my door always have a problem, a reason they need to see me. No one comes to see a lawyer just for fun."

"That's a little depressing," Becky said with a frown.

Catherine smiled faintly. "I don't know why I chose a profession that forces me to always take sides. Maybe I'm not a fighter and I'm just beginning to realize it."

"Is that all there is to it?"

Catherine took a sip of tea. Becky had always been perceptive. "Basically, I've lost confidence in myself," she said softly. "And I've become disillusioned with what I do for a living."

"Tell me what happened." Becky poured herself more tea.

"A woman came to me distraught over her divorce and the fact that she wanted full custody of her child, a little boy. She said her soon-to-be ex-husband would be a terrible father, that she just didn't know what would happen if he became the custodial parent and on and on. The woman said she feared for her son's safety and mental well-being. She was so convincing that I took her case and we won."

"And that's a problem? Would you rather have lost?"

"In this case, yes. I was so blind, Becky, I don't know what happened to my intuition. I would have passed on the case if I'd known I'd misjudged the woman entirely. I fought hard so that she could have her son." Catherine nervously folded and refolded a napkin.

"There's nothing wrong with that. It was your job."

"But I discovered later that what she really wanted was to hurt her ex-husband. She played me for a fool and used her son as a pawn in her game."

"Some people are consummate liars. That's no reason for a smart, wonderful attorney to leave her profession."

"I didn't say I was quitting entirely," Catherine pointed out, "but I was burning out. I've been offered a chance to teach, so I've taken a sabbatical."

Becky nodded sagely. "Seems reasonable."

"As it turns out, the timing is perfect. There's a lot to do now that Gram is gone. For one thing, she and Will Tanner did a pretty good job of tearing up Hope House. I need to oversee putting it back together."

The expression on Becky's face was abruptly full of mischief and delight.

"Why are you looking at me like that?" Catherine had seen that look on her friend's face more than once. It usually involved Becky trying to do some matchmaking or a prank in which Catherine wasn't interested.

"I'm just thinking about what a good-looking man Will is. Scrumptious, don't you think? Yum."

"If you want to describe a man like a baked Alaska or a cherry pie."

"Totally delicious, that's Will. Every single woman in town has taken notice. He's a great guy. Everybody likes him." Becky's eyes narrowed. "He's tall and gorgeous besides. He's eligible, Catherine…."

"Enough already!" Catherine put her hand up as if to stop the onslaught. "Yes, he's nice. Yes, he's good-looking but he's already taken."

"Not so," Becky protested.

"As far as I can tell, all his love goes to that little boy."

"That's not the same."

"He's not going to do one thing to jeopardize that child's welfare and that includes bringing a new woman into his life right now."

"But maybe that would help his case."

"I believe that his sister-in-law, Sheila, would be willing to twist any romance of Will's into something she could use against him. He needs to be cautious."

Becky grinned. "You could be right. Too bad. You would have been a perfect couple." Her eyes danced, and then she changed the subject. "When would you like to start working at the shop? I've got tons of displays to set up and I know you have an artistic eye. Why not come by tomorrow? Some things I purchased at an antique doll show arrived this morning. Wait until you see the china doll with blue glass paperweight eyes…" Becky was off and running on her favorite topic.

The next morning Catherine headed directly to Becky's Attic. She strolled through the shop, admiring some of the new crystal pieces Becky had just put out. She saw a few fingerprint smudges on some of the glass. Shoppers had, no doubt, handled the pieces. She felt the urge to get a soft cloth and start polishing.

She paused at the door to the back room. "I thought I'd check and see if you needed any help today."

Becky was on her hands and knees studying the contents of a large shipping container. Ten pairs of eyes stared up at her from inside the box.

"Porcelain dolls' heads," she said. "Very old and very beautiful. Some doll collector is going to go crazy over these. I know someone who might buy them all."

"If you ask me, it's a little creepy," Catherine said, joining her friend on the floor. "All those little faces staring up at you."

"Do you want to unpack them for me?"

"I could polish your crystal and silver pieces, if you like."

"Better yet. I'd much rather play with these dolls." Becky beamed at Catherine. "See? I knew we'd be a good team. I'm not taking you away from something at Hope House, am I?"

"Actually, you are, and I'm sure Will Tanner thanks you for it. You've gotten me out from under his feet so he can work in peace."

"Coffee?" Becky scrambled to her feet and reached for two mugs on a shelf.

"How will we get anything done if we sit around drinking coffee?"

Becky looked at Catherine pityingly. "You aren't in the world of high-pressured attorneys anymore. This is the benefit of living in a place like Pleasant. If anyone comes to the store before we're done, we'll give them a cup of coffee, too."

"I suppose you're right. Small town versus big city, city versus country. All I know for sure is that I have to pull myself together and move on."

"What's so great about moving on?" Becky, dressed in jeans and a soft yellow sweater, sat on a chair and curled her legs beneath her. "This seems like a pretty good place to me. Besides, you have Hope House here, your home."

Catherine didn't have an answer.

Becky must have read something in her expression

that Catherine hadn't meant to reveal. "You don't have to change everything all at once, you know. Give yourself time."

Before Catherine could respond, the shop's front door chimed. Becky peered through a peephole in the wall to see who had entered.

"Regina Reynolds," she said with some surprise. "Since when does she like antiques? She must be staging an older house."

"Excuse me?"

"Regina's a real-estate agent. She sells practically every house that goes up for sale in town. Sometimes she'll stage a home—decorate it appropriately so that a buyer can see how it could look if they chose to buy it. She doesn't usually need antiques, but maybe today…"

"Real-estate agent?" Catherine cut in, interested. "Is she good?"

"She's persistent and she has her ear to the ground all the time. If she hears someone might possibly, someday, maybe sell their home, she'll show up asking about it for weeks, months or even years. She's the same way with buyers. She never gives up."

Catherine tucked that bit of information into the back of her mind.

"I'll introduce you." Becky waved Catherine to follow her.

"Hi, Regina, I've got someone I'd like you to meet."

Regina Reynolds had the cool, assessing eyes of a predator. Catherine could see why Regina might be good at her work.

"Catherine Stanhope? Abigail's granddaughter?" Regina's eyebrows lifted and there was curiosity in her eyes. "I'm sorry for your loss. Are you staying in Pleasant long?"

"For a while. My grandmother started some renovations on Hope House that I need to see through."

"And then?"

Catherine felt herself hesitate. "I'm still exploring my options."

"Will you be keeping Hope House?"

Becky was right. Regina was a real-estate agent right down to the marrow of her bones.

"That remains to be seen," Catherine responded vaguely. Now that she was pressed for an answer, she felt a little less sure.

Regina pulled a business card out of her pocket. "Just in case you ever decide to sell it, here's my number. It's a spectacular house."

"True, but it's located in a rather out-of-the-way area, isn't it?"

"Not for the right buyer." Regina smiled.

Catherine was reminded of a shark again. "Really? If I were to sell the house, what would its value be? And who on earth would want a house that size in a town like Pleasant?"

"It only takes one, you know. Frankly, shortly after Abigail died, someone asked me about Hope House. I told them they were exceedingly premature, but I kept the name and number. If you ever decide, I could probably get you…" And she dropped a figure much higher than Catherine had anticipated.

"Enough business talk, ladies," Becky interjected. "Regina, tell me what you're looking for and we'll find you the perfect thing."

Regina willingly changed the subject. "I need to fluff up an old Mission-style house. It's much too stark to show right now. Nothing too fancy, of course, but feminine. It's currently too much a man's house…." With that, Regina stepped from her role of real-estate agent to her role as home stager and Becky flew into action, pulling knickknacks off shelves and tossing out ideas.

Catherine's mind spun. The house would probably sell for a good price. She could put whatever funds she got from it into an endowment in Abigail's name, something that would keep her memory alive in the community.

Before she could get much further with this idea, a mental picture of Will patiently replastering the wall with care and diligence, and of Charley sitting in the living room reading the bird book like a little man came to mind. It was their home, too, but she could hardly keep a huge house for one stranger and his nephew to live in. Will could find another home for himself and Charley, one that Sheila would approve of. Or perhaps the new owner would let him rent the guesthouse.

Despite the growing guilt she was feeling she needed to keep it to herself until she decided what she should do. If Regina Reynolds knew that she'd even considered letting go of Hope House, she'd be circling like a vulture, hoping for first chance at selling it.

It made matters worse that she liked Will Tanner more and more as the days went by. She'd have to be made of stone and ice not to. Will was incredibly good-looking, but that wasn't what appealed to her most. It was the tender, gentle way he cared for Charley and for the patience he displayed with the small boy's curious questions. Will was unflappable where the child was concerned—kind, caring, thoughtful...and Christian. The man practically came with Abigail's seal of approval.

And there was Charley who needed a loving home, a father and no more wrenching loss. A sigh escaped her. The complications were enormous. And Catherine had no easy solutions.

Chapter Eleven

Will felt as if he had one foot nailed to the floor and was going in circles. He needed to get the bathroom floor done, but there was the dumbwaiter to install and that gaping hole in the wall to repair. Plus, the new vintage-look stove was supposed to be delivered soon and he had to make space for it in the kitchen.

Catherine's work on the wall had caused him a bigger setback in just a few hours than any he'd had the entire time he'd worked for Abigail. If she helped him much more, it might jeopardize the entire project.

Still, he needed a place to put the stove, so despite all the other jobs to be done, he headed for the kitchen.

Emma was knocking on the door when he reached the lower level.

"Hi, Emma, what can I do for you?"

"I found some lovely lace doilies Catherine's great-grandmother made for my grandmother. I wanted to ask her if she'd like them."

"She's not here at the moment. She went to Becky's."

Emma cast him a knowing glance. "How is it going? You and Catherine, I mean?"

"Okay, I think. It's hard to tell."

"Just don't give up on her too easily," Emma told him enigmatically. "Sometimes she takes a while to come around."

"I don't understand."

"Catherine and Abigail were two of a kind—strong willed, stubborn, compassionate, willful and kind. If you can handle Abigail, you can get along with Catherine just fine."

Will stared at the older woman, half amused, half confused. "Emma, did Abigail say something to you about Catherine and me before she died?"

"Never mind, dear. Let's just say you and her granddaughter came up a lot in conversation." Then she smiled an old-lady smile and the wily expression on her features faded away. "Have her call me about the doilies." Without another word, Emma walked out the door.

On the way back to Hope House, Catherine heard someone call her name. She turned around to see

Jerry Travers, in a business suit, tie askew, trotting toward her.

"Hey, there! What's the rush?" she asked the red-faced man as he caught his breath.

"Too much work to do and too many places to be. Have you thought any more about coming to work for us?"

"I haven't ruled it out, but I really can't right now. Hope House has to be pulled together first. Besides, I'm occasionally helping Becky at the antiques store. I know you and your father have a great firm. I even heard about Travers & Travers's work down in the cities, but if I did do any work for you, I wouldn't argue cases."

The big man looked disappointed. "Okay, but the job offer still stands. I'd take any help you wish to give. I might even take a summer vacation if I knew I could leave things in your capable hands."

"You'll be the first to know if and when I'm ready."

"I suppose I'll have to settle for that. All I can say is, you'd better get Will Tanner to hurry up."

"I'm trying, Jerry. I really am." She thought she was being encouraging but it didn't seem to be helping much. "Some days the man moves like molasses."

Perhaps that was why she lost patience when she walked into the kitchen and found the old stove and two cabinets in the middle of the room and Will Tanner sweating and gulping water at the sink.

"Will, pretty soon there won't be a place in the house that's not torn apart!"

He put the glass on the sink and gave her a steely, appraising look that she felt right down to her core.

"Catherine, I'm doing the best I can." He spoke slowly, as if she were Charley. "I know that's not good enough for you, but it was more than good enough for your grandmother. Pushing harder isn't going to get things done faster. In fact, so far it's slowed things down. So if you don't mind, I'll go upstairs and work on the dumbwaiter."

"Just so you know, you are really annoying me right now," Catherine said. She had her hands on her hips and her feet firmly planted on the floor as if she was ready and willing to do battle. "I want this house done, not more torn up! What about that don't you understand?"

He strode up to her, his body rigid with aggravation, and met her gaze with cool, assessing eyes.

She put her chin out defiantly and held his gaze. Had she gone too far?

Much to her amazement Will touched her cheek with his forefinger and smiled at her. When she tipped her head up to look at him, he surprised her with a gentle kiss. "Cool it, little red hen. The sky is not falling."

Then he moved away and took the stairs two at a time.

She touched her lips where the memory of his kiss lingered. It had brought with it a jumble of emotions that bewildered her. She'd never before experienced a kiss she'd enjoyed so much—or had less likelihood of repeating. "Oh, Will…"

It was all very confusing.

Maybe she should try to see things from Will's perspective for a change. With a sigh, she left Hope House and headed toward Emma's. She'd stay there again tonight. It seemed wise to stay out of Will's way for the rest of the day.

Catherine awoke with a start. She rolled over to look at the clock by the bed. It was 1 a.m. She'd been dreaming but couldn't recall what she'd dreamed that woke her. She wanted—needed—to sleep in her own bed soon. Despite the dust and chaos, she would move into Hope House tomorrow, Will or no Will.

Unable to go back to sleep, Catherine pulled on her jeans and a sweatshirt and headed for the front door. Here in Pleasant she could take a walk in the middle of the night and be perfectly safe. She'd made dozens of midnight prayer walks during her visits to Gram over the years and tonight she needed fresh air to clear her head.

The night air could only be described as silky

as it caressed her skin, and the inky soft blackness of the sky made her feel as if she were shrouded in velvet.

"Lord," she began in a soft but audible voice, "here I am again. What do You want me to do? I'm a blank canvas right now for You to write on. I'm not hearing You very well. There's lots of static in my life right now. Could You speak a little louder? And what about Will's kiss?"

She strolled past the gazebo in the town square and admired the twinkling white lights strung inside the gazebo roof. That had been Abigail's idea. Leave it to Gram to bring light wherever she went.

Catherine looped around the block, and without consciously planning it she found herself walking toward Hope House. As she neared, she noticed a light in an upstairs bedroom. Will should have checked the lights before they left the house. When she saw movement inside the bedroom a small gasp escaped her and she backed up against a large oak. Then a familiar figure moved in front of the window. Will.

What on earth was he doing at the house at this time of night?

Without a key, Catherine had no option but to ring the doorbell. In a moment, Will's footsteps were pounding down the stairs.

He opened the door slowly, suspiciously, until

he realized who was on the other side. "Catherine? What are you doing here? It's 1 a.m."

"The question is, what are *you* doing here? Why aren't you at home with Charley?"

He didn't look good. His eyes were red-rimmed and he'd been running his fingers through his hair. It stood on end, powdered with plaster dust. "Charley is sleeping in one of the guest rooms. I didn't want to leave him at home alone. I'll just carry him back when I'm done here."

Catherine pushed past him, mounted the stairs and entered the bedroom she'd worked in the other day. She stopped suddenly. The plaster wall she'd dismantled had been restored. Only the tidy hole Will had originally cut was open now, ready to be framed.

"This is what you've been working on all night?"

"I know you've been frustrated with the progress I'm making, so I thought I'd spend some extra time…"

A flush of guilt and embarrassment spread through her. "I'm the one that used that wall to vent my frustration. I didn't realize how much damage I was doing or how much work it would take to fix it. I'm sorry."

"No big deal."

"It's a huge deal! Thank you." She snapped her fingers. "I almost forgot that I have something to show you." She scooted out of the room and returned with her arms full of old picture albums. Some were thick with dust. "I found these in the attic. There's something in here I think you'll be interested to see."

She laid them on the plastic-covered bed, opened the top book and flipped to the middle. "There! See?"

Will picked up the book to study the picture more closely. It was of a construction project of some sort. There were three men standing by a framed-in doorway, staring at the camera. One held a hammer, another a saw, and behind them a bed frame sans mattresses could be seen. "Is this what I think it is?"

"Yes. My great-grandfather had someone photographically record the building of this house. There are several other pictures including the porch being put on and an old cookstove being moved into the kitchen. You're looking at the original door between these two bedrooms." She flipped back a few more pages in the album. "And here it is complete."

It was the same photo only this time there were no men and the bedroom through the door was decidedly masculine. The one wall captured in the lady's room, as Will had begun to refer to it, was covered with wallpaper of overblown roses and rampant vines and completely feminine.

"So it was as Abigail speculated." He breathed a satisfied sigh. "We got it right."

"You've gotten lots of things right, you and Gram," Catherine said. She had to tamp down the urge to brush back the lock of dark hair that had fallen over his eyes. He'd worked so hard for this.

"Are you excited?" he asked, "To know that your family home is coming back to life?"

"Frankly, Will, I'm not sure." She pulled up a paint-cloth-draped chair and sat down, mindless of the dust. "I'd be ecstatic if Gram were here with us right now. This was her dream come true."

"What's your dream?" He closed the book and propped himself against a ladder.

She was silent a long time before speaking. "I don't know anymore. For years it was climbing the ladder of success. Originally I couldn't think of anything more fulfilling to getting to the top of a prestigious law firm and using my talents to make a difference in peoples' lives."

"You did that."

"Yes. I'm glad I did, but I feel like that dream has been accomplished. I was so focused that it wasn't until I was already living the dream that I realized it was no longer enough for me." She hoped and prayed that teaching would fill the void that had developed within her.

She leaned toward Will. "What's *your* dream,

then? Beyond finishing this house and making Charley your true son?"

"Those are big enough, don't you think? And I don't feel like I'm anywhere close to reaching either of them."

"You will." Of that she felt confident.

"And beyond that? I'd say it would still be creating a home and family for myself."

"And when you're done here…" she ventured cautiously, curious as to what he would say.

"Granted, I'm not getting rich here, but I have plenty coming in from my portion of the construction business, even though I'm not hands-on right now. I can go back to it anytime I like."

"Really?" That bit of information startled—and relieved—her.

"I chose to stay here—in Pleasant and at this house—because I wanted Charley to be exposed to a different life. Your grandmother was part of that. She taught him more in six months than any of us could have done in a year about having good manners, making wise decisions, respecting his elders and believing in God. I would never have known how to do that."

"Those were Gram's specialties."

Will shuffled his feet and looked embarrassed. "In a way this house and this place *are* my dream." Then he smiled wearily. "I'd better get Charley into his own bed. You should get some sleep, too.

Morning comes early around here." With that, Will disappeared into one of the bedrooms and emerged carrying the little boy.

Charley's cheeks were a rosy pink and his tousled hair in spikes. His small body was utterly limp against Will's shoulder. His long dark lashes fanned over soft round cheeks, a sleeping cherub.

She followed them down the stairs and out of the house, then locked the door behind them. What was it about this pair that touched her in ways she'd never before experienced?

"G'night," Will said softly as he moved toward the guesthouse. She could hear bone-aching weariness in his voice.

Catherine's head felt as though it would burst with conflicting emotions as she walked back to Emma's. The depth of Will's commitment to Abigail was far deeper than she'd first expected, and his passion for Hope House—well, she just didn't have it. Frankly, his dedication and loyalty put her to shame. All she'd wanted was to get rid of the house.

Had she approached this all wrong?

At Emma's she crawled into bed but lay there a long while as sleep eluded her.

Will had a difficult time waking up. He'd been running on empty by the time he got to bed last night and morning had come far too soon. Why

Catherine had been out walking so late, he didn't know, but he hadn't meant for her to catch him working at the house. She had enough on her mind.

He wasn't sure why he felt so protective of Catherine, but she generated in him a feeling similar to the one he had for Charley. He wanted to defend them both against the world. Catherine, of course, would rally from the loss of her grandmother, but Charley still had a lot of years to be vulnerable.

Will had thought of himself in many ways, but knight in shining armor had never been one of them. From a wild, impulsive youth to a hard-working man running a construction business to handyman and Christian, his life had taken lots of turns he hadn't expected. And now there was Catherine, who was turning his life upside down again.

He recalled the sweet taste and heady scent of her when he'd kissed her. What had made him do that, he wasn't quite sure. All he knew was that he'd like to do it again.

He made his coffee strong and dark, hoping that a jolt of caffeine would keep him going and, more importantly, knock thoughts of Catherine out of his mind. The woman was his employer and landlord, not exactly someone with whom he could have a casual liaison and walk away if it didn't work out.

He poured cereal into a bowl and sat down at the table to eat. After a moment he realized that he was staring out the window, lost in thought, filled spoon halfway to his mouth. She'd landed a hook in him somehow, he realized, and he couldn't get loose. Too bad, since it was apparent that Catherine hadn't even been fishing.

By late afternoon, Catherine and Will had almost completed the new bathroom floor. Truth be told, it was Will who had laid the flooring, but he'd told her she was a great help toting boards, running for lemonade and checking on Charley. Will's approval warmed her.

The prefinished oak gleamed in the late-afternoon sun as she cleaned away construction dust. "It looks good," she told Will, who was squatting on his haunches peering at his near-perfect workmanship.

"Wait until they bring the tub back. It's going to be amazing. I wish Abigail were here to…" His voice trailed away.

"Me, too." Without thinking, she rested her hand on his shoulder.

The warmth and power of sinewy muscle startled her, but she didn't draw away. Instead, she fought off the strange feeling in her chest. This man affected her more deeply than she liked. Surely these tender feelings for him were rooted in his close relationship to Gram. But that kiss…

Will looked at her with a gentle smile. "I don't

know about you, but I could use a glass of lemonade to wet my whistle."

They walked side by side, arm brushing arm, to the house, neither of them moving away from the contact. Catherine found a tray and Will loaded it with an icy pitcher of lemonade and two glasses. Without speaking, they worked in harmony, as if they knew each other's moves in advance.

Will and Catherine sat on the back porch in rocking chairs sipping their drinks and staring out at the lawn. Charley and his friends were playing a ruleless game of croquet where hitting the ball through the hoops seemed immaterial to winning.

"It seems to me we should do something to celebrate," Will finally said. "I feel good after seeing those pictures you showed me. We're definitely on the right track toward restoring the house. What do you think?"

Feeling lazy and content as a house cat lying in the sun, Catherine almost purred. "Sure. How should we commemorate the occasion?"

"How do you feel about riding the Ferris wheel?"

She sat straight up in her excitement. "I love Ferris wheels. I haven't been on one since I was a kid."

"There's a carnival coming through Hetland tomorrow. It's nothing big, but it's just right for

Charley's age. I told him he could bring a friend and he asked me if I was bringing one."

"And you picked me? I haven't felt this good since I got picked first for a baseball game in sixth grade."

"Don't go getting a big head over it," Will teased. He reached out and rolled a golden strand of hair around his finger. "You're just the prettiest friend I have. Besides, most of the others have wives who never like it much when I ask their husbands to come out and play."

Catherine smiled.

"We're leaving at five o'clock so Charley can have hot dogs and cotton candy for supper."

"I'll be ready."

The next day, Catherine was dressed and beginning to check her watch when Charley ran from the guesthouse to the big house to get her.

"Come on, Ms. Catherine! It's going to be great! Do you want to go in the house of horrors with me?"

"Hmm, we'll see, Charley, but I will have a cotton-candy eating contest with you, if you like." She picked up her purse and followed the boy to Will's pickup truck.

Will and Charley's friend Mikey were waiting for them. Charley scampered onto the cab's narrow back bench and immediately started a conversation with Mikey. Catherine hoisted herself into the front seat beside Will.

Will was dressed in tight, faded denims, battered but polished cowboy boots and a white shirt, collar open, sleeves rolled back. He took her breath away.

She smiled at him, hoping that he couldn't see how flustered she was by his appearance. This was the guy she'd imagined when she was drawing all those hearts on her notebook in junior high.

They didn't talk on the way to the carnival. Charley and Mikey took care of that for them. At the entrance Will bought them a string of tickets, gave them orders about what they could and couldn't do and reminded them that he'd be watching their every move. That didn't seem to bother the boys. They ran directly to the bumper cars and got in line with a bunch of other boys their age.

"They'll be there all evening," Will predicted, "trying to ram each other out of the park. Watch and see."

"And what will we do?" Catherine asked. She was more excited than she'd been in a long time. She loved the smell of popcorn and hot dogs, the sound of children laughing and the bright, moving lights of the rides.

"I'm thinking about that Ferris wheel. I can watch Charley and sit close to you at the same time. What do you think?"

"Let's go."

She could have ridden for hours, circling high into the sky and then plunging back toward earth. It didn't hurt that Will's arm stayed firmly around her shoulders or that she enjoyed the way the wind moved the dark hair off his forehead.

"You're right. We can see everything from here. Charley's still on the bumper cars."

"He'll be there till we go home."

They exited the Ferris wheel and walked from one end of the small midway to the other, holding hands and laughing at the spiels of the carnival barkers. Finally they stopped in front of a booth filled with enormous teddy bears.

"Hey, buddy, I bet you can hit that target with this 'ere baseball. If you can, you can win the little lady a big 'ole bear."

Catherine tugged on his shirt. "It's okay, Will. You don't need to. It's rigged, anyway."

Will eyed the target and the baseballs. "Have you ever had someone win something for you at a game like this?"

"No," Catherine said, laughing. "It's every teenage girl's dream to walk the midway with a handsome guy and a big fluffy teddy bear. She'd be the envy of every other girl her age."

"Then tonight is your lucky night." Will laid a number of dollar bills on the counter. "Let me see those baseballs."

"Please, don't waste your money." She tugged at his shirt even though deep inside she still felt a little bit like that teenage girl she'd once been.

Will tested the balls in his hands, deep in thought. Finally, he picked one. "Now watch." The ball hit the target dead center and lights flashed and a bell began to ring.

The man behind the counter produced a small teddy bear. "Here you go, lady."

"The lady wants a bigger bear."

The man grinned at him, showing them his lack of teeth. "Then you've got to hit it again. Only way to win one is to keep doing it."

"See, I told you not to waste your money."

"Darlin', I don't consider this a waste." The ball left Will's hand and again the bells began to ring and lights flashed.

The man exchanged the small bear for a slightly larger one.

The process went on for some minutes—one ball, one hit, one bear bigger than the last. After a while they began to draw a crowd. Will hadn't missed a single shot.

"Okay, mister," the booth attendant said. "This is your last shot. If you hit that, you'll get Goliath over there." He pointed to a brown-and-black creature at least five-feet high, a bulky teddy bear, with a disproportionately large head.

People began to cheer and Catherine noticed

people she knew from Pleasant grinning widely as one of their own wound up for another throw.

She felt her own excitement rising—and a memory of being a teenage girl longing for a handsome guy who would spend his money to win her a lavish carnival prize. It was an experience she'd never had—until now.

Thwack. People began to hoot and holler.

By the look of shock on the carnival man's face, he obviously had not expected Will to be dead-on again, but he was. Slowly, almost regretfully, he moved to take Goliath down from the ceiling of the booth and staggered with it over to Catherine.

"Here you go, lady. Yer boyfriend has a mighty good arm."

"It's huge!" she gasped. "The size of a real bear."

Will picked it up and wrestled it around until he had a good hold on it. "Do you want me to win you a smaller bear, too, so you have something to carry around?"

She felt light and young and playful again. Catherine felt tears threatening to fall from her eyes. No one had been this sweet to her in a long time— maybe ever. She was thankful Will couldn't see her getting weepy. Goliath was so huge his arms flapped around Will's shoulders and obscured his vision.

At that moment, Charley and Mikey came

running up to them. "You won that, Uncle Will? It's gi-normous!" The boys danced and dodged around Will's feet until Catherine thought he might trip over the pair, but he got to the truck in one piece.

"Goliath will have to ride in the back," Will told her. "I'm not sure he'd fit in the cab anyway." He looked at his watch. "Time to go, kids. Hop in."

With a few protestations, the boys did as they were told and by the time they were five miles out of town, they were sound asleep, smiling in their dreams.

"I hardly know what to say about you winning Goliath for me. It's a good thing I have a big house to put him in," Catherine said, grinning.

"Goliath could have his own bedroom," Will suggested. "There are plenty."

Catherine laughed, and it felt good. This entire evening had felt more than good. It had been wonderful. "How did you get to be so skilled at throwing a ball? You were pretty impressive."

"College. I was a pitcher. I considered going into the minors for a while but thought the band sounded better. Pitching was a skill I never thought I'd find another use for, but it worked out tonight." He flashed an even, white grin at her in the dimness of the cab.

"Thank you for a perfect evening."

He glanced at her, startled. "You consider *this* a perfect night?"

"Pretty close."

"Lady, we've got to do something about your lack of experience with perfect nights."

Catherine sighed and rested her head against the backrest. "Bring them on."

The next day, all that had happened the night before seemed like a dream. She'd gotten out on the wrong side of the bed—literally—and stubbed her toe on the iron leg of a table.

She went to the mailbox to get the mail she hadn't picked up the day before and brought it into the kitchen of Hope House to read it. The return address on the first envelope was familiar. It was from the real-estate agent she'd hired to sell her condo.

After reading the note, she crumpled the paper in her hand.

The condo had sold.

A door seemed to slam shut in her mind. One more break from the life she knew. One more anchoring rope chopped away.

The second piece of mail was a newsletter from the law office. They sent one out quarterly just to the staff, telling of the accomplishments of the firm, announcing office parties and picnics and generally motivating people to keep up the good work. Catherine opened the brochure and read.

Ted Chesterton named partner. So he'd gotten the position that could have been hers.

Office's summer outing will be held in the Wisconsin Dells. She'd always loved the Dells.

Three new babies have arrived since our last newsletter. She didn't even have a husband.

She crumpled the paper and threw it toward the basket, missing it. Catherine didn't move to pick it up.

What had she been thinking to walk away from all of that—a powerful, well-paying job, a beautiful home, a familiar lifestyle? And now she was here, in a mausoleum of a house, trapped into completing what her grandmother had started.

Then she remembered Goliath. At least she was likely the only one in her office with a teddy bear the size of a Volkswagen sitting in her bedroom.

She spent much of the day feeling sorry for herself, knowing it was foolish but doing it anyway. The cold reality of what she'd done was far less comfortable than the familiar life she'd left behind. For the first time, Catherine felt scared. What if everything she'd done was wrong? What if everything was a mistake?

Then she realized she had to let God take control. She'd chopped everything from her old life from beneath her. God was the only One she had to lean on now.

* * *

Will came downstairs for a drink of water and Catherine offered him lemonade on the porch. "Charley is going to stay overnight at his friend's house tonight," Will said. "Normally I like having him at home with me, but today I don't have much energy left for parenting. I'm not even sure I could make dinner."

"I hear you," Catherine said, leaning the back of her head against the floral headrest on the rocker.

"What do you say to grabbing something to eat? Then neither of us will have to cook."

"Pleasant has never been known for its fine dining," Catherine pointed out, "although the Pleasant Café makes a mean meat loaf."

"You haven't heard of Little Eddie's, then?"

"What's that?"

"Little Eddie's is about fifteen miles from here, out in the middle of nowhere. Apparently Eddie got out of the navy where he was a cook, moved into a house he'd inherited and opened a restaurant on the lower level. He's never advertised, but word of mouth has made him the busiest hot spot in the county. I took Abigail there once and she loved it."

Normally, Catherine might have hesitated, but if he'd taken Abigail there, she wanted to see it. "Sounds good to me."

"I'll have to call and see if I can get a reservation."

"To eat at a farmhouse in the middle of nowhere?"

"Like I said, it's popular. Besides, it is named Little Eddie's not because Eddie is little—he's almost six foot four—but because the eating area is small. No use driving over there if we can't get a table."

"Sounds good to me," Catherine said.

"Wait until you taste Eddie's cooking. You'll never want to go back to the overpriced, snooty restaurants in the city."

It occurred to Catherine that already she didn't want to do that. Just because this felt like a respite now, it didn't mean that it could be her sanctuary forever. It had never occurred to her while she lived in the city that someday she might enjoy the country enough to stay there.

But she *was* enjoying it, she realized. The cozy, quirky, everyone-knows-your-business life was pleasantly intrusive and she loved becoming reacquainted with the people from her childhood. She'd stepped inside a bubble when she'd arrived in Pleasant, one that kept her from the realities of city traffic, litigious clients and noise pollution.

Catherine felt herself reviving already. The prospect of an adventure pleased her enormously.

* * *

As Catherine rode with Will to this mysterious destination, an unexpected thought occurred to her. Despite her years in the city, she was still a country girl at heart. She liked pickup trucks. They were high off the road, large and powerful. And this particular truck held the pleasant hint of men's cologne, leather and fresh wood.

"I'm glad Eddie had an opening," she said as they took gravel roads cross-country toward the restaurant. "I wouldn't want to miss this."

"You sound like this will be your only chance." Will glanced at her, a puzzled expression on his face. "You're going to be here awhile, and Eddie isn't going anywhere. He's got a little gold mine in that place of his."

But her plan *wasn't* to be here indefinitely. Catherine just wasn't ready to tell Will that quite yet. Even though she was enjoying herself for now didn't mean she could live here permanently. The problem was that she saw how much Will counted on making his home at Hope House because of Charley. She closed her eyes and tried to blank out the thought of the cute little boy playing on the lawn.

She couldn't help it. No one in their right mind would expect her to live in Pleasant, right? Certainly not Lucy and her other friends from the law office. Granted, there were Will and Charley, part-time jobs and good friends, but there was also a house full of memories.

She knew better than to hitch her wagon to Will Tanner's star. He would do whatever was best for his nephew and that might not mean staying in Pleasant. And what would a woman with a Harvard law degree be doing working part-time in an antiques shop anyway? The whole idea seemed ludicrous.

Ahead, a few strings of white Christmas lights twinkled on a couple of scraggily pines. When they were near enough, Catherine saw a small, hand-lettered sign.

Little Eddie's
Open 5–10 p.m.
Call First or Plan to Wait

Eddie's restaurant-home, was a large white four-square house with black shutters and a green roof. Eddie had roped off a small area of gravel as a parking lot with black chain and iron posts. He'd also placed two large topiaries in clay pots on either side of the front door. It appeared nothing else had been done to announce that this was not simply another old farmhouse planted in the middle of rolling green fields. Through the curtained windows Catherine could see dim lighting and the flicker of candles.

Will opened the door and they stepped into the

house's entry. The woodwork was rich in detail and dimly lit wall sconces flickered around the room. The oak floor was dotted with jewel-toned rugs that had seen many footsteps over the years. The sophisticated, yet somehow shabby look was just right for the old house. It felt as though she were stepping into someone's private home.

A tall, muscular man emerged from the dimness. He wore black trousers, a chambray shirt and a pristine white apron. "Hi, Will," the man said. "Good to see you."

"I've brought you a new customer, Eddie. This is Catherine Stanhope, Abigail's granddaughter."

Eddie studied her for a long moment. "I see the resemblance." He smiled and the fierceness of his features softened into a delighted grin. "Abigail was a great woman."

Catherine felt a lump forming in her throat. Was there anyone her grandmother had not affected? "Yes, she was. Thanks."

"You're in luck tonight. I've got grass-fed beef, free-range chicken, corn on the cob, new potatoes and green beans. If you want seafood, I'd recommend scallops, although I prefer to eat what's grown around here rather in an ocean hundreds of miles away. I'm a locovore at heart."

Eddie waved them in.

They entered a large square hall, off which were several rooms. There were four tables with white linens in the living room of the house, and two larger ones in the dining room. All were filled with diners wearing everything from suits and dresses to jeans, polos and sweatshirts.

"The parlor is open," Eddie said and pointed them through a door toward the right. "I had a cancellation right before you called."

Catherine noticed Will and Eddie exchange a wink. When she walked into the parlor, she understood.

The room was painted a deep hunter green and the windows were hung with heavy velvet drapes in the same color. Flickering candlelight glowed at the single intimate table set with fragile old china and finely cut crystal. There were fresh flowers on the table, linen napkins and crystal salt cellars. It was as lovely as the table settings Catherine saw in magazines. Gold-framed mirrors, ornate wall sconces and an elaborately carved sideboard all made the room more elegant.

Catherine turned to Eddie. "I've never seen anything quite like it. How…why…what made you think of this?"

"I've always enjoyed cooking—even a couple hundred pounds of potatoes at a time while I was in the navy. After I got out of the service I spent some time going to cooking school. Then, last year I inherited this house from my great-aunt and -uncle. I wanted a change and decided I'd give this a try.

If it didn't work, I wouldn't be out much and if it did, I thought it might be fun." Eddie grinned. "I'm having a better time than I ever expected. I've got reservations into the middle of next month. I've had twelve men propose marriage to their girlfriends here, twenty-four couples celebrate their anniversaries and one wedding. The couple became engaged here and decided it would be right to have their wedding and reception here, as well."

"I can see why. The ambience is out of this world."

"I have my sister to thank for that. She's an interior decorator. She told me what I needed to do and went with me to auction sales to find dishes and furniture." Eddie shrugged his big shoulders. "I was glad to get back into the kitchen, I can tell you that. In fact, that's where I should be right now." He pulled out a chair for Catherine, handed them menus and disappeared as quietly as he'd come.

"I am completely blown away," Catherine admitted. Eddie was an unlikely chef in an improbable restaurant and it had turned out all right. If Eddy could go against what was expected and succeed, why couldn't she? The idea of bucking the norm was not one Catherine entertained often, but tonight it left her nerves tingling.

A young woman entered the parlor with a pitcher of water and a basket of bread. "Have you decided what you'd like to eat?"

"How about telling Eddie to surprise us?" Will said. He turned to Catherine. "Unless you aren't *that* adventurous."

"Surprise us," Catherine instructed the girl.

When the waitress had left, Catherine smiled awkwardly at Will. She twisted her fingers together nervously in her lap, out of Will's sight. This was beginning to feel unnervingly like a date.

Did she mind? Catherine wondered as she tried to sort out her feelings. The answer was surprising even to her. She rather liked it.

Chapter Twelve

The candlelight made Catherine even more lovely, Will observed, as it etched the shape of her face in light and shadow. The lightest strands of her hair glinted gold and framed her face in a beautiful aura. She'd lost some of the fine tension lines around her eyes and across her forehead since she'd been helping him. Whatever her impetus to leave the practice of law and return to her hometown, it had taken a toll on her.

He liked it when she smiled. Her eyes sparkled and her features grew radiant. It would be difficult for any man to resist. Will realized that for him it was becoming downright impossible. One kiss and he'd nearly gone off the deep end. He'd better watch it. He didn't need one more thing to complicate his life.

The young waitress reappeared carrying their salads. As she set their plates on the table she whispered conspiratorially, "I just helped someone propose."

"No kidding?" Catherine said.

"Did you see the couple in the far corner of the dining room when you came in? The guy came here this morning and gave Eddie the engagement ring he planned to give his girlfriend tonight. He told Eddie to think of a way to present it that would surprise her."

"How sweet. What did Eddy do?"

"Eddie made them tiramisu and put a single ladyfinger on top of her serving—with the ring on it!" The girl appeared enormously pleased by the idea. "Get it? Ladyfingers? A ring for a lady's finger...."

"Very clever," Catherine said, "and romantic."

The server's head bobbed in agreement. "I hope I find a guy who thinks of things like that."

"Hold out for him," Catherine advised. "He's out there somewhere."

The girl walked away thoughtfully.

"Is that what you're doing?" Will asked. "Holding out for Mr. Right?"

She hesitated before answering.

"You don't have to answer. It was a very personal question. I'm sorry."

"I don't mind. Until I heard those words come out of my mouth, I didn't realize that's what I really believe."

"Oh?" he looked confused.

"I've worked with women who said they were waiting for Mr. Right and yet were critical of every man who crossed their paths. I always thought they were judgmental and a little naive. After all, there weren't any blue ribbons on them either."

He smiled knowingly, as if he'd run into a few of them himself.

She absently toyed with her salad. "But that's not the same as waiting for God's guidance, is it? It's simply not smart to step into a relationship just for the sake of having one, right?"

"I believe that's wise." A smiled played around his lips but he sounded somber.

She looked up, her gray-green eyes studying him. "How about you?"

"I agree with you now," he said, "but I wouldn't have a few years ago, before I became a Christian. Then I thought that the only thing guiding my life was me."

Catherine's eyes widened and he felt himself redden. "I have to admit I was a pretty lousy guide, too."

"What do you mean?"

"The years I spent with the band are almost a blur to me now, like they happened to someone else, someone I don't even know. Once I was running my own company, I grew up."

"We all do," she said gently. "None of us start

out like we want to end up. Gram always pointed that out."

His expression darkened. "But it wasn't until my sister got sick and I met Abigail that I really began to get my head on straight." He looked down into his nearly empty salad plate. "I'm not proud of that, Catherine. I was wild, rebellious and reckless. People thought I was successful and a lot of fun, but I knew I was empty inside."

He lifted his head to look at her. "There's no way I can tell you how grateful I am that God made a new man out of me."

Will probably didn't realize that his admission had stirred Catherine in a way that a litany of his triumphs and successes could not. She'd been around brash, self-important men, lots of them.

Will was a refreshing change. She'd lived in a unique solar system these past few years. It was good to get out and see what else was in the universe.

Then that quixotic, romantic spell that Eddie's little place seemed to weave fell over them, as well.

The easy camaraderie she felt with Will was remarkable, Catherine mused as they ate. It was not just everyone with whom she could eat in companionable silence and feel completely comfortable. Usually she felt the need to fill empty space in a conversation with small talk or idle chatter. Not so with Will. Every word had meaning, as did every silence.

"Tell me more about your sister." Catherine had a burning curiosity about Charley's mother. Maybe it was because despite all her problems and short-comings she'd managed to raise a delightful, well-adjusted child.

Will's eyes took on that hazy, faraway expression they always did when he was thinking deeply. "Annie was the middle ground between my brother and me. Part of her was passive like Matt and another part of her personality was a bit of a rebel, like me. I'm not sure it was an easy combination. Annie wanted to be good so badly, but her propensity for doing daring things finally led her to drink, I think, although I don't know how she got started initially. I'd already left home when that began. She was one of those people for whom alcohol was poison, one sip luring her into a morass from which she couldn't escape.

"Annie was the most loving, tender, vulnerable and sweet person I've ever known." Will's features suffused with pain. "Maybe, in some way, she was doomed from the start. Doomed, at least, from that first taste of alcohol."

"I'm so sorry." Catherine's heart ached for this woman who could inspire such love in Will.

"Me, too, but she raised an amazing kid despite

her problems. Charley has all of Annie's good traits, but as far as I can tell, none of the weaknesses."

"Annie must have had a lot of wonderful qualities to raise a boy like Charley."

He toyed with his coffee cup. "That's why I don't want Sheila and Matt to take Charley. Their personalities are so different, so unlike Annie's or mine, that I'm afraid they'd try to shape him into their mold."

Catherine nodded but didn't speak.

"Sheila is all about success, money, achievement and status," Will continued. "Charley is about putting baby birds back in their nest if they've fallen, about comforting his friends when they get hurt and sharing what he has with anyone who needs it. He's all heart, they're all head. That environment would crush him."

"I know what you're saying," Catherine said. "All too well."

"Annie wanted me to care for him and I promised her I would." His finely chiseled jaw hardened and his eyes grew stony. "Or I'm willing to die trying."

It was after eleven when Little Eddie appeared in the doorway holding their bill. "Are you guys ready for breakfast yet?" he asked jovially. "'Cause if you aren't, I'm going to have to send you home and tell you to come back tomorrow night."

Catherine glanced at her watch. "Where did the time go?"

Will jumped to his feet to help Catherine from her chair. "Sorry about that. You aren't going to be any good to me tomorrow as a hired helper if you're tired."

She caught him by the sleeve as they made their way to the truck. "Will, I'm no good to you as a hired helper at all. I've made more work for you rather than less. I'm sorry."

He grimaced. "I haven't exactly been the best teacher either." Then the look he gave her made her heart thump harder in her chest. "We'll both do better tomorrow."

"I'd like that very much."

She must have dozed off on the ride home, Catherine realized. The last thing she remembered was looking at a sky full of stars. When she awoke, they were sitting in the driveway of Hope House, and Will was looking at her much as she'd seen him look at Charley—tenderly and with deep affection.

Catherine struggled awake. "How long have we been sitting here?"

"A half hour."

"And you've been watching me sleep? Why didn't you wake me?"

"I enjoyed it. Besides, you look like you needed every bit."

He *enjoyed* it? That was exactly what her

grandmother said on the occasions when Catherine had awoken to find Abigail by her bed, hands folded in her lap, a smile on her lips, watching her sleep. Those were some of the times Catherine had felt most loved.

This woman had snagged his heart, Will thought ruefully. He wasn't quite sure how she'd done it, reserved as she'd been at first. He'd let his guard down. There was nothing he could do about it now except pretend it hadn't happened.

He had two goals in life. To make Charley his legal son and to complete Abigail's dream for Hope House. Those two dreams meshed. Living at Hope House for at least two more years gave him a real home for Charley, a good home with vast gardens, gazebos to play in and friends nearby. Here he could be a stay-at-home dad, always on the property, always around for the boy. There was nowhere else he could do that, Will knew, and it was an important part of his argument to keep Charley. Once custody was established, he'd feel much freer, but until then, Hope House was the perfect solution.

Sheila and Matt were never home during the day, and they stayed busy most evenings as well with entertaining, fundraising events and the theater. If Charley lived with them, he would be raised by a string of sitters and live-ins.

Will couldn't be deterred from his goal now.

Impulsively, he leaned toward Catherine and brushed his lips against hers. They were soft and warm and her breath tasted of the chocolate-covered strawberries they'd had for dessert. Her blond hair tickled his cheek and she automatically turned her face to his like a seedling seeking the sun.

Sleepily she lifted her arms and slid them around his neck and pulled him closer. Will put his arm around her back.

Seconds later, Catherine's eyelids flew up like a window blind and a cold dash of reality splashed over them both.

Will pulled his arm away and she dropped her hands to her lap.

"I'm sorry, I…"

"No problem. I shouldn't have…"

They stared at each other in the dim green light of the dashboard.

Will cleared his throat. "A perfect end to a perfect night. Thank you, Catherine."

"Thank *you*." She grabbed for the door handle.

Will was immediately out his door and dashing around the truck to her side. He caught her in his arms as she scrambled to the ground.

She put the palm of her hand against his cheek and he could feel the warmth of her. Then, as suddenly as it was there, it was gone.

Chapter Thirteen

"Hey, Ms. Catherine." Charley came through the back door of the house, his hair still damp from his morning shower.

"Hey, Charley. You're up early."

"Watcha doin'?" He took the chair beside hers and stared at the piles of papers Catherine had accumulated there.

"I'm getting things ready to drop off at the bank. What is Will doing?"

"He said I had to entertain myself while he ordered some stuff on the phone."

"Do you want to come with me?" she offered, amused by the little boy's apparent boredom.

"You bet. I'll tell him." Charley darted out the door.

By the time she had her papers together he was back. "You're supposed to send me home if I'm any trouble," Charley informed her.

She smiled at him. "I'll keep that in mind, but I'm not too worried. Let's go."

Walking down the street and looking through the eyes of a child was a different experience for Catherine. There were more bugs and birdsongs than she'd ever imagined. They spent much of their time looking at the clouds, trying to decide what the puffy white shapes reminded them of—a bull, a clown or a coffeepot.

They got to the bank just as its doors opened for business. As they passed through the open foyer that faced the tellers' windows, Charley pointed at an oversize framed portrait of a stern-looking man with a trim mustache and fuzzy sideburns.

"Who's that?" Charley asked, his eyes wide with curiosity.

"That's my great-grandfather. He's the one who built Hope House. He also started this bank."

"Wow!" The boy stopped in the middle of the floor and stared up at the likeness.

Taking advantage of his fascination, Catherine quickly dropped off the papers and turned to go. "Ready, buddy?"

Charley turned to her with a look of awe. "You must be important if he built your house and started this bank." He turned around looking at the marble floors and high windows of the old building.

"No more important than you are, kiddo."

Charley studied her for a moment. "Is that what

being humble is? Uncle Will says when you don't think you're a big shot and you really are, you're humble."

Will was really covering all the bases in raising this child, wasn't he? That man needed to be this little boy's permanent father. There was no way Charley could get a better one.

As they stepped outside, Catherine didn't see Regina until the woman was almost upon them. She was carrying a thick burgundy-colored briefcase and looked very businesslike in her bright yellow suit.

"Hello, Catherine."

"Hi, Regina. Going to the bank?"

"Yes. I'm doing a closing there. I sold the sweetest little house to a couple from southern Minnesota. They're very excited about relocating to Pleasant."

"I'm glad you're keeping busy." Catherine wanted to get away but didn't care to be impolite.

"Have you thought any more about…" Regina glanced at Charley standing next to Catherine and added, "you know what?"

"What, Catherine?" Charley pulled on her hand. "Thought about what? Is it your birthday? Uncle Will says that's the only time a person can keep a secret. Otherwise he says it's very bad."

"No, it's not my birthday, honey. It's something private between Regina and me, that's all."

"Oh. I wish it was your birthday. We could make you a cake!"

Catherine grinned at Charley, and waved good-bye to Regina, happy to escape her curious eyes.

As Will removed the mail from the mailbox the next afternoon, after Charley had left to play with Mikey, he saw Catherine walking toward Hope House, her hands in the pockets of her khakis, her gaze cast down. She moved with her shoulders curled forward as if the weight of the world were resting there. Her feet were dragging, scuffing the concrete with a small shuffling noise. What was on her mind?

In the days she'd been here, Catherine had softened. She was no longer so reserved and questioning. In fact, when she smiled at him, he felt as if a light had been turned on somewhere in the room around him.

"Hi, Catherine," he called out and watched her lift her head. Her eyes brightened at the sight of him. The swelling of pleasure in his own chest surprised him. It had been only Charley's smile that could do that to him—until now. What would it be like to see her every day? "How was work?"

"Better than a day at the law office, that's for sure. I polished crystal, played with dolls, arranged vintage hats and planned a tea party. How about you?"

"They delivered the bathtub today. It's back in place and I'm almost done with the plumbing. You should be able to give it a trial run soon."

She rubbed the small of her back. "Sounds wonderful. Let me know when I can get in."

"You look preoccupied. Did something else happen?"

Her hesitation was so brief that he could have been imagining it.

"Two things. When Charley and I were at the bank we ran into Regina Reynolds."

"That's a woman on a mission, for sure. I've always had the impression that business comes first with Regina."

"I got that impression, too, but she seems nice enough."

"Probably. I don't know her well. I've never had a house to sell in Pleasant. I've heard she's pushy as a bulldozer in clay. But you said two things happened."

"I stopped in and said hello to Jerry Travers and his father. They have a nice office—homey and comfortable. It's very agreeable."

"Enjoyable enough to work there?" Having Catherine employed in Pleasant would make him breathe a little easier, assuring his and Charley's security. Because of Abigail's death, he'd found his life suddenly entwined with hers. It wasn't a bad thing, though. Being with Catherine was one of his favorite activities these days.

"They asked me the same thing. It feels too soon to make any big decisions."

He held out his hand. "Come see the bathtub." She put her own hand in his and allowed him to lead her inside.

As they entered the upstairs bath, Will held his breath. He wanted this to be good. He'd wanted it so much, in fact, that he'd even sent Charley to the drugstore for bubble bath and a loofah to put on the tub tray to make it more appealing. Charley, giddy at the prospect of buying presents for Catherine, and with Mikey's mother's help, had come home with a large pink bottle of soap with bright pink flowers floating in the liquid, coordinating body lotion, a sponge on a stick and a small gift book entitled *The History of the Bathtub*.

Will had let Charley arrange it as he wanted. The boy had even found a bud vase and filled it with one large pink peony and laid a pile of fluffy white towels on a small stool next to the tub. The boy was, Will mused, going to make a wonderful husband someday.

Catherine gasped with pleasure at the sight.

The tub had been restored to its original splendor, and Charley's little display looked surprisingly right.

"It's gorgeous! Better than I've ever seen it before!"

"That's the point of restoration, to bring it back to good as new. Do you like it?"

"I love it." Catherine turned to him, her eyes shining. "Who did the bubble bath?"

Will felt his cheeks grow ruddy. "My idea but Charley's execution. He did okay, didn't he?"

"You are amazing. Both of you. It's charming. Thank you."

"It's nothing more than I would have done for Abigail." He cleared his throat. "Except, maybe, the bubble bath stuff."

It was sweet to hear laughter peal from her.

"I believe I owe you an apology, Will." Her eyes were wide and suddenly somber.

"What for?"

"For doubting you. I have to admit that I thought you and Gram had concocted an unnecessary scheme. I thought Hope House was fine as it was. But this is lovely."

"So you won't stop me from carrying out the rest of our ideas?"

"No, I won't. Just promise that I don't have to live in the mess forever. Work as fast as you can, okay?"

"Fair enough," Will said, but his thoughts were not on the house, but on a pair of bright eyes smiling at him, and her hand that was still enclosed in his.

Chapter Fourteen

Now she'd gone and done it. She'd agreed to let Will restore Hope House the way he and Abigail had planned. What had come over her?

It was the beauty of Will's work and the tender touches Charley had added that had weakened her resolve. She was stuck in a tug-of-war between her guilt and her determination to move on. At least she'd told him to hurry. His work would give her some time to decide if she wanted Regina Reynolds to sell the house for her or turn it over to a larger real-estate agent. It would also give her a chance to truly unwind, to have a little fun at Becky's shop and even to help Jerry Travers clear out his backlog of cases. What she knew for sure was that she couldn't allow Will to take two years to finish it. She would insist that Will hire outside workers to assist him, as many as it took.

She'd given herself a little time and space. That

was probably a good thing. Catherine ran her hand over the marble counter in front of her. As of this moment she was ready to keep the house just so she could soak in that glorious bathtub anytime she wanted.

The house phone rang, jolting her out of her thoughts.

It was her friend Lilly Marks from the Three C's law office. "How are you doing up there in nowheresville? Are you bored yet?" Lilly's lilting voice was filled with laughter.

"Actually, no, not at all." Catherine sounded a little surprised at herself.

"It can't last, you know. You'll tire of all that nature and small-town camaraderie soon enough. I think you should come back here. We miss you terribly. Even the big bosses talk about your absence. 'When Catherine handled this case...' or 'Catherine always did it this way...' They'd have you back in a heartbeat."

"That's nice to hear, but they'd better not hold their breaths."

"Just wait," Lilly said confidently. "You'll get sick of that white elephant of a house, no social life and nowhere to eat but the Main Street Café. You'll be back. I'd dump the place so fast your head would spin."

"I'm sure that's true," Catherine said, battling her visceral response. The way Lilly so casually dismissed Hope House and Pleasant was almost offensive. This was Catherine's home she was talking about! The house in which she'd grown up!

Why was she going to sell it if she cared so much?

Quickly Catherine turned the conversation to less volatile topics.

Almost as soon as Catherine hung up, the phone rang again. This time it was her aunt Ellen.

"How are you, Catherine? Are you coping with all that's going on there in Pleasant?" Ellen's voice was sympathetic. "I'm sure it's a good deal to manage."

"I'm plugging along. Thanks for calling. I needed to hear a friendly voice."

Ellen's laugh was low and husky in her ear. "The phone line travels both ways, you know."

"Touché. What are you up to these days?"

"I'm going to be in your area tomorrow taking some photos. I thought I'd let you know in case you were free."

"Photos of what?"

"I'm doing a freelance job for someone. Children. As long as I was in the area I thought perhaps you'd enjoy it if I took a couple of Charley."

"No kidding? Tell me the details."

Charley was willing and eager to go to the park with Catherine the next morning to meet Ellen. Will didn't even ask where they were going. A tribute, Catherine hoped, to the faith he had in her. Little did he know they were going to create a very special gift for him.

Ellen was so enthusiastic about Charley's rosy cheeks, silky hair and all-American-boy appearance that she barely had time to talk to Catherine. She was too busy posing Charley and looking at him through her lens to make small talk.

"I am so glad you brought him over!" she said as she finished the photo shoot. "These pictures are going to be fabulous." She glanced up at Catherine. "Do you think his father would consider having him model?"

"Doubtful," Catherine said with a laugh. "He doesn't even know we're doing this. I wanted to surprise him."

Ellen raised an eyebrow. "You must like him very much to do such a thing."

"He's the one who's been working on Gram's house. He deserves a thank-you gift from me."

"Why don't you get in a photo, too, Catherine. Go over there and stand by Charley." Ellen kept talking and clicking pictures. Catherine and Charley laughed together and made silly poses.

"One more. Will the two of you sit together on that stone bench? This place has amazing backdrops. Look at those trees, will you?"

As Ellen chattered, Catherine and Charley

studied a caterpillar that he'd carefully moved out of the way before they sat down. It crawled up the top of Charley's finger, and as Catherine bent over to study the two-toned creature, their heads met. For a moment it was as if Ellen didn't exist.

When she looked up, her aunt was smiling at them with a Cheshire cat–like grin. "What made you so happy?" Catherine asked.

"Just wait until you see these photos, Catherine. They're going to be amazing."

"All I know is that I appreciate you taking the time for us. Will should be delighted to have a portrait of Charley in his home."

"Like the one at the bank?" Charley asked.

"Not quite so large. And this one is a secret. Don't tell your uncle what we've done until Ellen sends us the proofs, okay?"

"I promise."

Ellen hugged Catherine as they prepared to leave. "That's one darling child. If the uncle is half as good…"

"It's platonic, Aunt Ellen." At least, that's what Catherine kept telling herself.

On the way home Charley seemed to be thinking about something.

"What's up, Charley? Why so serious?"

"I was just wondering if I could play with you when we get home. Mikey went to visit his grandparents and it's boring without him."

"All I'm going to do is look at my grandmother's dishes. That would probably be boring." She'd learned a lot from Becky about dishes and had come to appreciate just how fine a collection resided at Hope House.

"Not when I'm with you. Nothing is boring when you're around."

Catherine was so charmed by those sweet words that she gave him a big hug and a kiss on the cheek. The Tanner men were certainly winning her heart!

Once home, they settled themselves in front of one of the sideboards in the dining room and Catherine took a dish from the top of one stack. "They're pretty, aren't they? Look at this one. It's Flow Blue china and if you hold it up to the light backward you can see the blue color flowing through to the back of the plate." She held it up for his inspection, recalling when her grandmother had explained the same thing to her.

"Cool. Can I see another one?" He leaned closer.

Catherine felt the small warm body bump against her own. "Sure."

They'd gone through two cupboards when she heard Will's feet pounding heavily down the staircase.

Charley looked at her wide-eyed. "Uncle Will is mad," he said. "He never walks like that unless he's mad. He says he never raises his voice, so sometimes his feet talk for him."

Catherine suppressed a smile. That was more proof how hard Will was trying to be a good father. If, while he was taking apart this monster of a house and putting it back together again, the only thing loud about him was his feet, he was doing a pretty good job.

"I'll go check on him," she told Charley. "You go wash your hands and get an ice-cream bar from the freezer."

"Can I take it outside?"

"Sure. Help yourself."

Much to her surprise, Charley gave her an enthusiastic kiss on the cheek before disappearing into the kitchen. She didn't move for a moment but touched the spot he'd kissed with the tips of her fingers. They were trembling. This child was very easy to love.

Then she remembered the boy's uncle, who was now stomping toward the dining room. He didn't even see her as he walked through to the kitchen. His face was red and furious and he held an open letter in his hand.

When Catherine followed him to the kitchen, the letter was on the countertop. Will had braced himself against the counter and stood there staring at the floor.

"Will, what's wrong?" Catherine moved toward

him, wishing she could smooth the lines of misery
from his expression.

He glanced at her and the expression in his eyes
was pure torment. He looked as if he'd aged sig-
nificantly in the past few moments. "Sheila's gotten
herself an attorney."

He nodded toward the open letter and Catherine
picked it up.

This is to inform you that I am now represented
by the law firm of Zack, Jackson & Reed. They
will be handling for us the adoption of Charley.
I know you will try to fight this, Will, but I recommend that you do not. Matt and I can provide
a far more stable environment for the child and
have the wherewithal to provide for his education at the finest schools. Were Annie alive, I
know she would approve of this. Anything you
do to fight this will only hurt either Charley or
your relationship with your brother, so please
consider your actions carefully.

My attorney will be in touch.

Sheila

"Sheila didn't see—or want to admit—how
well-adjusted and stable Charley is with me." He
slapped the heel of his hand against the counter.
"And what relationship with my brother? Something's very wrong with Matt. He's gradually grown

more distant over the years—toward both Annie and me—and in the last five months… It's got to be Sheila, doesn't it?"

He moved toward the table and dropped into a wooden chair. "Maybe I should have kept my mouth shut and not told my brother not to marry Sheila. At least then I would have the chance to see him occasionally. As it is now, Sheila won't leave us alone together in the same room."

"What does she have on him?" Catherine asked quietly. "She must have something she's holding over his head. Otherwise, I can't see why he wouldn't reach out to you no matter what. She's got a hold on him that is very powerful. There's got to be something behind it."

Will looked at her with interest. "You think so?"

"You knew your brother as a child. Would you have predicted that he'd behave this way toward you as an adult?"

"Not for a minute. We were best friends. I was older and always the leader. Matt is a follower by nature but he always had my back. I don't even recognize the man he is now. Of course Sheila rarely lets him talk—and never to me alone. For years Matt has acted like he's carrying a burden that's too heavy for him. You'd think he was a hit-and-run driver who felt guilty but was too afraid to confess."

"Perhaps Sheila isn't the bad guy at all. Maybe she is trying to protect him from something," Catherine said softly. "Maybe Matt is a hit-and-run driver concerning some area of his life."

Will looked shocked at the idea. "You think so? What could be that bad?"

"Maybe you should try to talk to him alone. Ask him if he really believes he and Sheila should have Charley."

"Of course he'd feel like that," Will said. "Charley is his nephew, too."

"He could still have a differing opinion." Catherine's voice grew quiet. "Maybe he doesn't think Sheila should be Charley's mother either." She scraped her fingers through her hair, "Or maybe I'm putting too many ideas on the table."

"I doubt Matt's version of things is any different from his wife's." Will sounded less sure of himself. "Sheila wouldn't let me near him to ask him anyway.

"My brother works from a home office. He moved it there at Sheila's suggestion. It's easier for her to keep an eye on him."

"Just a thought." Catherine could virtually feel the misery coming off this man in waves.

"And now she's got an attorney." He looked her straight in the eye. "Have you heard of the firm?"

"Yes, I have."

"Are they good?'

"Some of the best," she answered morosely. "Your sister-in-law is no dummy."

"What am I going to do, Catherine? How can I fight that?"

He wanted her to say she would help him, but it was obvious that it wouldn't come through her lips. He wanted her to go into attorney mode just long enough to ensure that Charley would stay with him. He'd listened closely to her ever since she arrived, but all he'd heard from her was relief to be out of her law firm and determination not to find her way back into it.

"You may have to hire an attorney yourself," Catherine said. "Sheila's obviously gearing up for a tough fight."

He'd work at Hope House for half price for the next two years if she would help him, but he wasn't ready to put her in the awkward position of having to turn him down, at least not yet.

He could read by the expression on her face that Catherine knew what he wanted from her. He also knew she wasn't interested in getting back into the fray. How far did he dare go before she rejected him, them, entirely?

Chapter Fifteen

The next day Catherine had to get out of the house, away from Will. Will's every expression, even his body language told her that he wanted her to represent him in court. To still her circling thoughts, she took a walk and ended up on Jerry Travers's doorstep.

"Well, look who's here!" Jerry appeared happy to see her. "Did you come to work?"

"You're incorrigible, Jerry." She gave the big man a hug.

"I've been called worse." He waved her into his private office, a room lined with leather-bound books on cherry-wood shelving. She took the chair across the desk from his.

"You don't know me like you used to, Jerry. Maybe I'm not such a wunderkind anymore."

"You? You've got to be kidding me. What's wrong, Catherine?"

"I'm tired, that's all. Bone weary, exhausted, drained. It wasn't until I got to Pleasant and slowed down that I realized the pace I'd been keeping. I had a couple of cases that nearly drove me into the ground, so I decided to quit my job and sell my house. Then Gram died. Now I find myself making decisions and then second-guessing everything." She ran her slender fingers through her thick blond hair and scraped it away from her face.

Jerry calmly laced his fingers together and rested them on the desk. "I'm no clairvoyant, but as a small-town attorney, I have had a lot of practice at reading between the lines. Let me guess."

"Go ahead," Catherine said, not really expecting him to understand.

"It wasn't the pace in the city that got to you but one of those cases you mentioned. Every attorney has at least one, or will have one before they retire—a case they regret taking. Those are the ones that bother you like a missing tooth. You keep sticking your tongue in the empty spot until it drives you crazy."

He had her attention now.

"It's not the small decisions about your grandmother's estate that get to you. You can handle all that. What troubles you are the emotional decisions that only you can make."

"That about sums it up. You're good, Jerry."

He chuckled, and that cozy, teddy-bear look

returned to his features. "That's what happens when you are a general practitioner rather than a specialist. I don't practice just one kind of law, so I never know when my client walks in what he or she wants to see an attorney about. Perhaps they come in for estate planning and eventually admit they want to know if they can afford another child. Or someone says he's concerned for Grandpa's welfare but really wants to know if he can get his inheritance early. There's usually more than one agenda if you look deep enough."

"Because you're so smart, maybe you can help me."

"I'm willing to try. Tell me about the case that's troubling you."

Catherine willingly obliged. It felt good to talk to someone who understood the judgment calls that needed to be made every day, the discernment it took to tell truth from lie and fact from fiction. As she spoke, Jerry nodded understandingly, as if he'd walked in similar shoes.

"I had an ugly case, Jerry. One in which the child's parents were fighting bitterly over their little boy. The mother was my client and she told me some pretty alarming things about her husband's relationship with the child—neglect, harsh punishment, all the stuff you don't want to hear."

"And the problem was?"

"I bought it all, as Gram might say, hook, line

and sinker. I played right into the woman's hands. I did everything I could to make sure she had full custody of that child."

"That's what you were hired to do."

"But not at the expense of the child. Ultimately had the mother been happy to have her child? Maybe, but not as happy as she was to see that the ruling stuck a knife into her ex-husband's heart. The little boy was just a pawn in a chess game to her, Jerry."

"You can't be so sure…."

"I helped the wrong person gain custody and an innocent child paid the price for my error. That's why I wanted to leave the firm. I lost faith in my own judgment. It's why teaching law appeals to me now. I can't hurt anyone if I'm not hands-on. And if God's trying to tell me something and I'm supposed to go in another direction, so be it."

Jerry opened his mouth to say something but Catherine rushed on.

"I wake up at night wondering if that woman might damage her little boy emotionally. Thanks to me, at the very least he's a likely candidate for boarding school and long-distance parenting. I read the situation wrong, Jerry, otherwise I would have passed on the case. I should have known…."

"When I went to law school they didn't have a class on mind reading. Maybe you did. I know you went to Harvard Law. You really should get something more for all that tuition you paid."

"Don't be silly." She smiled in spite of herself.

"That's exactly what I'm telling you. Don't be silly. What's done is done. You did what your client asked and you learned something that will help you in the future. I know about the battle that your grandmother waged for you. Maybe you're too wrapped up in this because of your own situation."

"You're right. I did see myself in that child." Catherine felt a load lift slightly from her shoulders. "That's why it pained me so."

"And the child will still see his father, correct?"

"Yes, of course."

"Then I have a hunch he'll be less scarred by this than you are."

"Thanks for putting things in perspective, Jerry."

"You're welcome. Your bill will be in the mail," he said cheerfully. "What's the other decision you have to make?"

"You will have to bill me if I take any more of your time."

He dismissed that with a wave of his hand. "Nah, my last appointment canceled. Something about a sick cow. It's hard to live in the fast lane, isn't it?"

"I am enjoying Pleasant's 'fast lane' but it's also

the problem." She told Jerry about her quandary— to sell Hope House, send Will and Charley packing and get on with her life, or to keep it and be saddled with it indefinitely.

"Is it so bad to be 'saddled' with a spectacular mansion in a beautiful setting?" Jerry sounded genuinely curious. "Is this even a problem?"

"It is if I'm teaching somewhere else. Plus, I want to be done with responsibility for a while. I need to take a break and then move on. All that I cared about most is gone now."

"We all may want to be done with duty and accountability, Catherine, but if you shed one job, another will take its place, you know that. What you are running from will follow you. You're looking for something that simply isn't realistic, I'm afraid."

He was right. She was intentionally running away from her career, from her duties and her dissatisfaction with life. Maybe it was for the best that she'd given Will time to work on the house. The time it took might be worth it. After all, her mind and heart needed a little mending, as well.

She took her time walking back to Hope House. She would do something that took her mind off everything. Something she hadn't done in a long while. The first thing she would do when she got to the house was look through Gram's recipes.

* * *

"Want to take a break?" It was late afternoon when Catherine poked her head into the room in which Will was working. "I just made a chocolate cake—from scratch. There's plenty of cold milk to go with it. And put both feet on the ladder, you're making me nervous!"

Will scrambled down the ladder. "This is perfect timing."

"Good. I hoped so. It's already set up in the gazebo."

She surprised him at times. Catherine was like watching the moon on a cloudy night. Sometimes she was bright and easily discernible; other times, the clouds with which she was struggling hid much of her luminosity from sight. This afternoon it was the former. Her smile was wide and beautiful and the frown lines that sometimes etched her forehead were nowhere in sight.

He followed her to the pergola where she'd set out enormous pieces of cake on china plates, a cold pitcher of milk and Abigail's good silver.

"I'm not accustomed to such service. I usually eat over the sink and drink out of Charley's used tumbler."

"Don't tell Sheila that." She poured his milk and then sat, tucked her hands beneath her chin and studied him.

"What are you staring at?" he finally asked, after devouring the cake in a few bites.

"You. I'm trying to figure out what makes you tick. You're so patient with Charley and me."

"It's not hard to be patient with people you care about."

And I care about you, he wanted to add.

"It's more than that, Will. It's your demeanor. It's as if you, and I'm sorry if this sounds sappy, glow with goodness."

He coughed. "Me?"

She laughed and handed him a napkin. "It's true."

"It's not me, Catherine. It's God in me. Matthew says, 'You are the light of the world. A city on the hill cannot be hidden.' That's the only 'glow' I have."

He stood up and held out his hand. "Let's take a walk."

As they moved around the gardens, he began to explain. "When I first came to Pleasant and met your grandmother, I noticed something in her, too. She had a serenity and calmness about her that was practically unearthly."

"Yes, I know. I saw it, too."

"Granted, she could be feisty and funny and a real pain in the neck if she wanted, but her inner tranquility blew me away. It wasn't until she started talking about her faith that I began to catch on."

Their walking slowed until they paused by an old oak that had been there as long as Hope House— or longer.

"She told me that God changes a person from the inside out." He heard his voice catch a bit as he spoke. This was a deeply emotional conversation for him. "Anything you see on the outside of me is a result of what God's done for me on the inside."

He watched her consider his words. Catherine looked particularly vulnerable right now. Fragile and beautiful.

"Will, I don't feel very in tune with God these days. I have a lot of questions I'd like to ask Him, but I'm not sure I know how anymore. I haven't been giving God the time He deserves."

He chose his next words carefully. "For me, hearing God is like a…knowing. Something inside me grows still and very much at peace. It's the peace that tells me God is giving me His answer. I've never done anything that I wasn't fully at peace about that turned out well. I don't move forward without that sense of rightness in me anymore. And I check it out in Scripture. It's a great handbook for life. Your grandmother taught me that. Maybe instead of keeping busy, you should just sit still for a while and listen."

She slowed her steps, and as she looked at him she wound a strand of hair around her finger, as if that might help her solve her puzzle. "Just sit?"

"The last month of Annie's life I was caring for both her and Charley. Sometimes I'd find the quietest place I could and sit there until I felt God's presence. After some time with Him I could go on refreshed and clear. I can't explain it—I just know it happens that way." He felt exposed talking like this. He was still a new Christian, and he still had a lot of learning to do. He didn't feel ready to be telling Catherine how to live her spiritual life.

She gazed at him so intently that he felt disconcerted. What was going on behind those beautiful gray-green eyes now?

"You speak from the heart, don't you?"

"There's really no place else, is there? At least not if you are going to be honest."

To his surprise she winced a little, as if he'd sent out a dart and it had landed somewhere painful.

Quickly, Catherine changed the subject. "I have an errand to run. I'll be back later, okay?" She squeezed his hand and gave him a tremulous smile. "Thanks."

Catherine escaped to the only place she could think of, the back corner of Pleasant's small library. Feeling lost, she opened the Bible she'd found in the stacks and hoped that Will's method worked. She was desperate for some heavenly guidance right now. Maybe He would speak first. The conversation had to start somewhere. Catherine turned to Proverbs 3. A single verse stood out on the page.

In all your ways acknowledge Him, and He will make your paths straight.

That seemed straightforward. She turned back to the Psalms and landed in the thirty-second chapter. *I will instruct you and teach you the way you should go; I will counsel you with My eye upon you.*

She was stunned by the clarity and the appropriateness of the verses. God certainly *had* started their conversation. Suddenly she didn't feel all that sure about the decision to teach that she'd made back in Minneapolis.

Acknowledge Me, He said. I'll put you on the right path and teach you what you need to know. Besides that, I'll keep My eye on you, Catherine.

She flipped back to Proverbs and read the preceding verses. *Trust in the Lord with all your heart, and do not rely on your own insight.*

She'd been trained to rely on herself and her instincts. But they'd begun to fail her and here God was, telling her it was time to trust in Him and Him alone.

But what if He gave her an answer she didn't like? What if His will was completely the opposite of what she planned to do? Then what?

Acknowledge Him. Trust Him. Don't rely on myself.

This wasn't going to be easy, not for an independent, stubborn woman, but something had to change. Putting her confidence in the God of the Universe didn't seem like such a bad idea right now—even if He did lead her on paths on which she hadn't planned.

Chapter Sixteen

Ellen's photos arrived at Hope House the next morning. Catherine immediately took them to Emma's house. She didn't want Will to find them.

The two of them huddled over the glossy black-and-whites and those in vivid color. There wasn't a bad photo in the bunch.

"These are my favorites." Emma pointed to those of Catherine and Charley hovering over the caterpillar. "Precious. You should order that one for Will. I think he'd like a picture of you on his wall, too."

"I'm temporary. I want something that he can enjoy permanently."

"Why couldn't it be permanent?" Emma asked, looking innocent as a newborn.

"You know why! It's because…because…" No good answer was coming to her although Catherine knew she had plenty, like the call she'd received from the law school yesterday asking if she'd be willing to pick up another class in the fall.

"Just think about it, dear. Sometimes God's plans and yours are not going to be in accord. I'd stick with His plans if I were you."

Emma studied her with a faint smile on her wrinkled face. "Do you know much about plow horses?"

"Not a thing."

"When they are working, they wear blinders so they can see only straight ahead. That way they will keep working without being spooked by something in their peripheral vision. You've been in blinders for a while now, but they've come off. It's time to look up and see what's around you."

Catherine considered that all the way back to Hope House. She was leaning against the kitchen counter thinking about the beautiful pictures her aunt had taken when Will entered the kitchen.

"Hi. I thought I'd be back sooner. I got caught at the lumberyard. I'm on my way home to feed Charley." He eyed two ripe avocados on the counter. "Did you know that I happen to make the world's finest guacamole? I worked in Texas for a long time and learned from the best."

"Let's make guacamole, then. If Charley likes it, that is."

He picked up two avocados and squeezed them gently. "This is going to be good."

While he chopped tomatoes, Catherine found a sombrero-shaped serving bowl and some tortilla chips. Occasionally they brushed against each other as they moved about the kitchen, working together like a well-orchestrated symphony, gliding easily from one task to the next without getting in each other's way.

Catherine set out plates. The only other times she'd felt this way had been when she and Abigail worked together in this very kitchen.

"You are a great deal like you grandmother," Will said, as if he'd read her mind. "She's the only other person I never stumbled over in the kitchen. My sister, Annie, told me I cook like I drive—I take my half of the road out of the middle…. Why are you looking at me like that?"

"Just a little déjà vu moment. I was thinking the same thing. Tell me about your siblings when you were growing up," Catherine encouraged. "Because I was an only child I was always fascinated how children could coexist in the same house. I never had to share. I took for granted that everything was mine, put there for me by adults. That backfired once or twice, particularly the time I decided to take the car for a drive when I was nine."

"You didn't."

"I did. First and last time, I guarantee you that. Abigail made it clear that she'd decide when I got an automobile, and until then I was to stay out from behind the wheel." Catherine chuckled at the memory. "I also had to wash and polish that car every Saturday for the entire summer as punishment. By the time the summer was over, I was so sick and tired of it that I didn't care if I ever drove again."

Will pulled up a kitchen stool and sat down, his long, denim-clad legs straddling the seat. "I was the problem child in my family, too. I had all the good ideas and talked my siblings into trying them with me."

"What good ideas?" Catherine poured them each a glass of sweet tea.

"Homemade wings, for one. I talked Annie into flying off the roof of the garage with them." There was impishness in his expression that was both charming and dangerous. "Fortunately, she didn't get hurt because she landed on Matt. He was so interested in seeing her fly that he forgot to get out of the way. He broke his collarbone cushioning her fall. And then there was that time I decided to clean the motor on Dad's car, an incident with the explosion in the kitchen and shaving the cats so they wouldn't shed. My mother had been complaining about hair all over the place, so I never did figure out why she wasn't happy that I tried to help her out."

"And where were Matt and Annie all this time?"

"Helping me. Annie was particularly eager to do whatever anyone told her to do." His lips twisted in a rueful expression. "I know Annie started drinking in high school. I never figured out who first encouraged her or bought the liquor." His fists clenched and unclenched. "I might have pounded the tar out of them if I had."

"And your brother, Matt?"

"He could stand up for himself if he had to, but he usually did whatever his buddies suggested. Thinking back, I guess I shouldn't be surprised that Sheila can boss him around. Everybody did."

"Didn't he hate it?"

"I suppose so, but he didn't say much. Matt withdrew sometimes and no one knew what was going on with him. He and Annie grew very close after I left.

"I'm not sure why my parents let him go so deep into his own shell. Now that I've got Charley with me, I realize that parents have to be vigilant every minute. Sometimes mine seemed oblivious to our antics."

They sat down and lingered for a long time after Charley bounded in, took half of what they'd prepared and retreated to the other room to watch television. Neither seemed to mind or inclined to break the spell of the moment.

"Do you want to come upstairs and see my progress?" Will asked. "Tomorrow I'm going to wrap up those bedrooms we rejoined so you can move out of the guest room and back into your own spot."

"And then what? Are you close to being finished?" Catherine tried to hide her eagerness.

"Hardly. You know how long Abigail's list is."

She approached the subject carefully. "Is everything on the list really necessary? There must be some things that are more important than others." *Things that don't have to be done so I can move on with plans for this house.*

"It was all equally important to your grandmother."

This wasn't going to be easy, especially if he kept invoking Abigail every time Catherine tried to think about finishing the renovations.

The phone rang early the next morning. Catherine thought about ignoring it. She hadn't had her coffee yet, but the jarring ring was persistent. She finally decided to pick up. "Hello?"

"Catherine?" a faintly familiar female voice said. "This is Regina Reynolds."

"Hi, Regina." Catherine closed her eyes. She'd hoped not to hear from the woman quite yet. It felt easier to put the house decision on hold. Hope House could sit empty until the right buyer came along. Catherine's sense of urgency had declined radically of late.

"Have you thought any more about selling Hope House?"

"Regina, I told you that I'd rather no one know that I'm even considering it right now."

"I haven't said a word, I promise, but the party I told you about called me again. Apparently it's a couple looking for a potential B and B site. They asked me how many bedrooms your place had and if the guesthouse was livable."

Catherine thought of the cozy home Will had made and something in her gut churned. "I have to think about this, Regina. I'm sorry."

"Don't think too long. These buyers are serious and they have already narrowed down their choices."

"Thanks for calling." Catherine hung up quickly.

Now why did I do that? Here it was, the perfect out for her. She could quietly sell Hope House and move on. Oddly, it didn't seem quite so important right now.

"I wish you hadn't introduced me to Regina," Catherine told Becky the next afternoon at the Attic as she checked a delivery against its invoice. "She's been calling and pressuring me to consider selling Hope House."

"Ignore her. You have to decide what you want to do. You have no obligation to give her what she wants."

"What do you think I should do?"

"Me? I just said it isn't Regina's business and it's not mine either."

"That's different. You're my friend and I'm asking for your input."

"My thoughts go in two directions, but I'm not sure which is the best."

"I want to hear them both."

With a put-upon sigh, Becky leaned back in her chair. "Part of me totally understands why you want to sell the place. You've never shown much interest in living in Pleasant, so I don't know why that should change now. The person you love most is no longer here. You crave a fresh start. Selling the house, cutting all ties and moving on is certainly that."

Catherine nodded.

"*But* would you regret it for the rest of your life if you sold your children's heritage?"

"My children? When did my potential children come into this?"

"You'll have them someday, you know. How could you bring the Stanhope legacy alive to them?"

That thought hadn't even occurred to Catherine.

"And the treasures you'd lose! I'm an antiques dealer. I know the value of what's in the house. It's a king's ransom, Catherine. I can't see you letting it all go."

If she were honest, Catherine thought, she couldn't either.

"I'd love to see you find a way to keep the heritage alive. That was what Abigail wanted. Won't you regret not fulfilling her dream?"

"But what would I do here if I kept the house?"

"What would you do somewhere else?"

She had no answer. She was like a little kid, shucking her clothes as she ran to the ocean, eager to jump in and not even knowing if she could swim. Maybe shedding her memories was like that—foolish and ill-advised.

"Teach for a while. I certainly know what I won't do—I won't practice law other than perhaps a little behind-the-scenes work for Jerry Travers just to help him out."

"Fine. Why don't you run away from your law practice for a while and make the decision about the house later. You'll have somewhere to live while you're deciding."

"You're so sensible, Becky."

"Thank you." Becky smiled beneficently. "Very few people have ever called me that."

It was three o'clock in the afternoon and Will was miserable. He'd attempted to block everything from his mind except the plumbing project he was engaged in, but nothing helped. There'd been another letter from Sheila and one from her attorney. She was forging ahead and making it sound like if Charley spent another day with Will, the boy would fall totally behind physically, educationally and socially. Sheila was behaving as if Will was methodically sucking the child's brains right out of his head.

A heaviness grew in his gut. He'd been thinking and praying about this but had never felt the need to take action until now. It was time. He had to ask Catherine if she would help him with his legal case and he dreaded it with all his heart.

He knew the odds weren't good, but he felt compelled to ask her anyway. Abigail had been very proud of her granddaughter and she'd told him many times what Catherine did for a living and how good she was at it. Abigail had also revealed times when Catherine's cases had gone awry. He could get someone else to represent him, he knew, but Catherine was the one who would understand this case from Charley's point of view. Because she had been through a tug-of-war waged by the adults in her life, she'd do everything in her power to protect Charley from the legal wrangling.

Nothing he told himself made him feel any better. He'd watched Catherine closely and she was skittish. This wasn't a woman who was accustomed to being wrong. The custody case she'd been involved in had affected her to the core.

He wasn't quite sure how to approach her. Still, Will had to try. He would do anything for Charley, including making a fool of himself and jeopardizing the tenuous friendship—though it had become far more than friendship to him—he and Catherine seemed to be building.

There was no use waiting any longer.

He caught her in the front hall when she returned from Becky's Attic. She was studying her reflection in the mirror.

"Do you think I look like the photographs of my ancestors? The elder Stanhopes, I mean?" She turned her face at different angles to scrutinize her features.

"You look like pictures of Abigail when she was young. And you have the same eyes and determined chin of your great-grandfather."

"How flattering," she said sardonically and moved closer to the glass.

"It is, actually. I've always looked at that portrait in the bank and admired his resolve and grit. You have those same qualities."

She turned to him. "Why, thank you."

"Unless, of course, one is on the wrong side of that resolve and tenacity."

She followed him into the living room and joined him on a couch. "What do you mean?"

"If someone asked you to do something that you didn't want to do, I could see you holding out forever, just on principle."

She opened her mouth and closed it again. "Where are you going with this?"

She was beautiful when she was confused and much less intimidating than when she wore that confident, self-assured legal-eagle expression that must have terrified her opposition in the court.

"I have a request, and I have a hunch that you won't like it. I know you've given up law and don't want to return. I get that. I also understand why you got so blown away by your child custody case. It was terribly painful for you. However, that's exactly *why* I have to ask you this question. Will you represent me in my fight to get custody of Charley?"

He watched emotions chase each other across her features—dismay, resistance and then sadness. Instinctively he steeled himself for her answer.

"I can't, Will." Her voice was barely a whisper. "I promised myself never again. I was at the top of my game and still blew it. I wouldn't be your best choice, not anymore. I'm so sorry."

"If not for me, how about for Charley? You were his age once. You know how it feels to have people argue over you when you've just lost a parent. He loves you, Catherine. You would be so good for him. You'd fight like a mother lion for him. I'm sure of it."

"I don't have that fight left in me, Will." Her voice was laced with exhaustion. "I'm all tired out."

"I'll do everything in my power to keep this place running so smoothly you won't even know it's here. I'll make sure there's no construction where you're working and sleeping. Catherine, with your experience, you could probably handle this without blinking."

This wasn't going well. Will tore his fingers through his hair. "Come on, Catherine, it's about *Charley.* I'm not trying to manipulate you. I just want to take care of my nephew like my sister wanted me to. Will you help me?"

Chapter Seventeen

Couldn't he see he was tearing her heart out? She'd told him she wouldn't practice family law anymore. Much as she might want to help him, she wasn't sure she could. That was the bottom line. Her confidence was gone. Even she didn't understand it. She'd lost cases before and had never let it bother her, yet a case she'd won had crippled her.

Maybe she was throwing the baby out with the bathwater, as Abigail used to say, by running away from everything. Perhaps selling Hope House was misguided, but one thing she knew with perfect clarity was that she was done representing clients.

"I'm sorry, Will, but I can't. I'll give you some names…"

He shot out of the chair. "I don't want names, Catherine, I want you! You of all people should know how it would be if he had to live with Sheila and Matt. You saw them. They make your own aunt and uncle look like Mr. and Mrs. Warm and Fuzzy. If you want to run away from something, fine. But I want to *save* something—a human being."

"Aren't you overdramatizing?" Even before the words were fully out of her mouth she knew they'd been a mistake. He wasn't being theatrical. In fact, he had a pretty clear picture of the pitfalls. She was the one being histrionic, but she was spent. Life had come down hard on her lately and she was worn out, depleted.

She wasn't surprised when he stormed out of the house. What she was surprised about was how bereft she felt after he left.

Will stormed back to the guesthouse, flung himself into the burnished leather chair in his small living room and leaned back. He felt as if his life was made of sand and it was slipping inexorably through his fingers.

He didn't get it. How could she turn him—and Charley—down? Or maybe the better question was, how did he have the nerve to ask her to help them?

She'd been crystal clear about her decision to quit practicing family law. She'd never equivocated. And yet he'd had to try.

He plopped his booted feet on the rough wood coffee table and sunk even deeper into the chair. Oddly, the part that hurt most, he realized, was that he'd overestimated the depth of friendship he and Catherine had developed. On some level he'd really believed that she'd come out of retirement for Charley—and for him.

I'm projecting my own feelings onto her. Maybe because I'm falling in love, I think she is, too.

He sat bolt upright and groaned.

It was love he felt for her—not tolerance or fondness, but love. At that moment Charley walked into the house with his buddy Mikey. "What's wrong, Uncle Will? Are you sick?"

"No, Charley, just a little frustrated with myself." He cast his gaze about for something to divert the child. "How about a snack? Are you guys hungry?"

"Yeah!" the children chimed.

As soon as Will fed the kids, he returned to Hope House to take his mind off the issues plaguing him. The bedroom wall and newly inserted door were complete and the rooms were ready to paint, but that wouldn't expend nearly enough of the pent-up energy he was feeling. He needed to use his muscles today and he knew just what to do.

Catherine found Will in the basement chipping the grout from between the hand-laid stones in the foundation. He'd braced the walls with thick lumber until it looked like sketches she'd seen of the construction scaffolding surrounding the ancient pyramids.

"What are you doing? Trying to tear the house down from the bottom up?"

"Repairing the foundation," he responded tersely, not turning to look at her. He kept on chipping at the grout. "Abigail requested it."

"Then let me help," she said. She picked up a chipping hammer and started working at the grout just as Will had done.

Hammering, as she'd discovered while removing the plaster wall, was the perfect task for expending built-up frustration. The next hour passed like an eternity, but when Catherine stepped back to study her work, she was surprised how far they'd come.

Taking a cue from her, Will stepped down from his ladder. "Impressive what one can do with an hour of silence and a lot of suppressed aggravation, isn't it?"

She smiled sheepishly at him. "Can we call a truce?"

"Agree to disagree, you mean?"

"Something like that."

"Maybe we won't be able to keep up the work pace if we don't stay angry with one another." Finally a smile played on his lips.

"'Do not be quick to anger, for anger lodges in the bosom of fools,' it says in Ecclesiastes," she retorted.

"Okay, then. Although I still disagree with you."

"You have that right. It's a free country." She was relieved he'd still speak to her. She hesitated a moment before adding, "Lemonade?"

She loved sitting on the porch with Will, gazing over the painstakingly groomed lawn and feeling the slight breeze move through her hair. She unclasped it from its ponytail and shook it out so that it tumbled down her back.

"As a kid, I never appreciated how calm and quiet it is here. I thought it was deadly boring." With one foot she moved the swing in which she was sitting.

"Most kids would. You have to mature a bit to value this."

Catherine nodded. Was that it? Had she begun maturing into a life in Pleasant?

"What were you like as a kid, Catherine?"

"That would be a dull conversation," she joked and tucked her feet beneath her.

"Not for me."

"I was a studious overachiever. I thought anything less than a four-point average or a perfect paper was unacceptable. I was on the yearbook staff, was statistician for the basketball team, class secretary and anything else that had to do with words and numbers. My entire social life revolved around church activities. And you know how awful I must have been at baseball. Borrring."

"Then you've been intense and serious all your life."

"You could say that."

"And rigid and unbending when you believe you're right?"

"Now that's going a little far. I follow the rules, of course, as everyone should, if that's what you mean."

"When you're at Becky's shop and you want to cross the street to the post office, do you cross in the middle of the street or go to the corner and cross at the stop signs?"

"That's a silly question." She squirmed, uncomfortable on the swing. She put both her feet flat on the floor. "Of course I…usually…almost always… go to the crosswalk."

"Even if there are no cars coming?"

Catherine felt herself blush. "Even if there are no cars parked there."

"I thought so."

She waited for him to say more but he didn't. He didn't have to. He'd already pointed out that she was serious and inflexible, a person who believed in rules and kept them and once she decided she was right, was difficult to convince otherwise. That wasn't exactly an easy cloak to wear.

"I know, Will, that it's difficult to understand why I can't…"

He held up his hand. "Don't say anything,

Catherine. I'm upset, I admit it, and disappointed. I'm also positive I can't get a lawyer with more experience and knowledge than you about a case like this, considering the fact that you went through it yourself. I thought our friendship would count for more."

She tried to ignore that. "Because I was recently on the wrong side of a case like this, I'm able to give you names of excellent attorneys…."

"I don't want them. I want you."

She drew a deep breath. "Will, we've already discussed this."

She could tell by his facial expression that it really wasn't okay but he was willing to remain silent to keep the peace. "Thank you."

Silently they returned to work. By the end of the day, because they'd had little to say to each other, they'd managed to remove the old, crumbling grout from one entire wall.

"How'd we do?" she asked.

"Just fine. Having you around made me stay on task. I wanted to show you what a hard worker I am."

"And I wanted to show you the same thing," she admitted as they walked up the stairs to the kitchen.

"A few more days of one-upmanship and we'll have this thing done."

"I'm stiff and sore already. I'm not sure I'll even be able to get out of bed in the morning."

As she stood at the kitchen counter washing her hands, Will came to stand behind her. He placed his hands on the counter, one on either side of her. She felt the warmth of his presence. Her hair brushed against the front of his shirt.

Catherine wiped her hands on a towel and pivoted to face him.

He was closer than she'd anticipated and she could feel his breath on her cheek. "Will, I…"

He lowered his head and gave her a gentle kiss. She trembled and he pulled away to study her face.

She could hear her heartbeat pounding in her ears. No one's kisses had ever affected her like Will's.

Shaken but trying not to show it, Catherine slipped beneath his arm and smiled back at him.

The grin he gave her told her that he knew exactly how he'd affected her. And that he had enjoyed it.

She had enjoyed it, too. She'd been trying to deny that she'd fallen for the man. She might whisk his home out from under him. That was not a good foundation for romance.

"Catherine," he leaned toward her, "I want to say something to you."

"Not again…."

"I appreciate the fact that you were straightforward with me about not wanting to represent Charley and me."

"But I…"

"I know that was hard, but I'm glad you didn't string me along and make me believe you might change your mind." He looked down at the floor.

When he lifted his head, his eyes were flashing. "Tell me anything but never keep information from me."

Catherine felt a little sick.

"Annie tried to hide her addiction from me and maybe if she hadn't, I could have gotten her some help."

"But she was sick…."

"Matt didn't tell me that he and Sheila had eloped until they'd been married more than a month because he thought I'd be angry. And Sheila…she's as secretive and cagey as they come."

He reached for her and held her shoulders so he could look directly into her eyes.

"Secrets are the one thing I won't tolerate. Everything bad in my life has involved someone keeping a secret." He flushed beneath his tan. "I felt like I should tell you that—and let you know that even though I don't agree with you, I appreciate your honesty."

"Will, I…"

He leaned back and crossed her arms over his chest. "Now what are we going to do about us."

"Us?" Catherine squeaked, even though she knew full well what he meant.

"You feel it. Don't tell me you don't." His smile grew lopsided. "You're different from any other woman I've ever met, Catherine. From what I can gather, you and I were polar opposites when we were young. You kept every rule with as much diligence as I broke them."

"That doesn't sound like a reason to…you know… want to be with someone. I was straitlaced, introspective and cerebral."

He moved closer. "There may be more to be said for straitlaced and cerebral than is common knowledge."

"What's in it for me?" she teased.

His eyes darkened and he lowered his head toward hers. Their lips had barely touched when the doorbell rang.

"We'll just ignore it," Catherine murmured. "Maybe they'll go away."

It chimed again, longer this time.

"We can't pretend we aren't here," he pointed out rationally. "We can be seen through the window."

Reluctantly she slipped from his arms. "I'm doing this under protest."

"Don't worry. We can pick up where we left off. I'll remember exactly what we were doing."

The huskiness in his voice caused a shiver of pleasure to run down her spine as she padded to the door and threw it open.

Before she could process what was happening, Regina Reynolds burst into the house waving a sheet of paper. "I've got an offer on this house, Catherine! It's even more than we discussed. Isn't that wonderful? I'm sure you'll have this albatross off your hands very soon!"

Chapter Eighteen

Regina nudged her way past Catherine and into the living room. "Oh, hello, Will. Nice to see you. I'm so sorry to barge in, but I just couldn't wait to tell Catherine the good news."

He was gaping at her, speechless.

"I suppose you knew that she was thinking about selling Hope House. Even though she hasn't given me the official go-ahead to put it on the market, someone came to me and asked me what I knew about the house."

She turned to Catherine, who remained stunned and frozen in the entry. "You remember me telling you about those people who want to start the B and B?"

"Yes, but…" Words were failing her.

"Well, they came back to me this afternoon practically salivating. They'd looked at more houses and said that nothing came close to your place. And they haven't even seen the inside yet!"

Catherine cast a desperate look at Will but couldn't read his thoughts.

Regina took a deep breath and plunged on. "You'll never get a better price than they offered. I can probably get even more once they see the inside. I'm sure they'll want the furniture, too."

"Furniture?"

"They're in the area for only a day or two, so we'll have to set up a time that they can come in for a tour."

Regina laid some papers on the nearest side table. "I know you're surprised and need time to think, so I'll just leave these here for you to study."

"But Regina, I'm not so sure…"

"Call me tomorrow, will you?" She laid her hand on Catherine's arm. "This is very exciting. I hope I haven't overstepped my boundaries, but I couldn't let this go by." She air-kissed Catherine on both cheeks, waved at Will and disappeared through the front door.

All the air in the house seemed to have been sucked out by Regina's pronouncement. Catherine could hear the clicking of the mantel clock thundering in her ears and her heart hammering in her chest.

She turned to Will, who seemed as staggered as

she was. Then Regina's words began to sink into his consciousness and his features darkened.

"You're going to *sell* Abigail's home?" he said, his voice incredibly soft and low.

"I just talked to Regina about it, Will." She wished he would yell at her. It would feel less disconcerting. "I didn't say whether I would or I wouldn't."

She recalled his words about keeping secrets and decided that full disclosure was the only way to go from here on out.

"I came to Pleasant with the intention of selling the house, but when I found you here and heard about Gram's plans, I didn't know what to do. You had the house torn up, so I had to put the idea on hold. And now, the longer I'm here, the harder I'm finding it is to consider."

"You kept the fact from me that you planned to use me to repair the house and then dump it?"

"Excuse me, but you *are* getting paid to do the work."

"You didn't care to mention it to me when one of the consequences is that Charley and I will lose our home?"

"You knew this was temporary!"

"How long was the charade going to go on? Or were you just going to knock on my door one day and tell me I need to be out by noon?"

His neck turned red and the heated flush bled onto his cheeks. He clenched and unclenched his hands by his side. She'd never seen someone look quite so angry and indignant, even after years in the courtroom.

"You, of all people, should know how it would be for Charley. Don't you realize that part of the strength of my argument to keep Charley is the fact that we live here?"

"It's not just about location."

"Here I have a home with space for him to play in a place he loves. Matt and Sheila live in a very urban area. He'd have to have someone accompanying him just to play in the park."

"You'd do a good job of raising Charley anywhere."

"I want to provide him with something better, Catherine. If you sell the house now, we'll have to move."

"Will, I..."

"Don't say anything, Catherine. Enough has already been said tonight."

He strode to the door in long steps. His body brushed past hers as he went for the door. Then he was gone.

Will blindly made his way to the guesthouse.

How could she keep that from him? How could she go against everything her grandmother wished for? And Charley...

How he hated secrets!

Will stopped at his front door and took a deep breath. In the course of twenty-four hours Catherine had refused to help him with Charley, virtually sold his house out from under him and shattered every dream Abigail Stanhope had ever had. And that didn't count using him like a puppet or making him feel like a fool.

He heard the back door of Hope House open. Before Catherine could call out to him, he slipped into the guesthouse, closed the door and locked it. There would be no more lies and feeble explanations tonight.

Inside, Will couldn't quit pacing. His mind was a virtual carousel of repetitive thoughts. Thankfully Charley wasn't home to see him like this.

Not knowing what to do with himself, Will walked into the bathroom, stepped into the shower fully dressed and turned on the water. The icy blast on his head was like a slap in the face—miserable but useful for interrupting the obsessive thoughts racing through his brain. There was a time in his younger days when he would have punched his fist through a wall or slammed a chair into another piece of furniture.

Now, however, things were different. He was not a child of man but a child of God now.

Catherine awoke on the couch in the living room where she'd cried herself to sleep the night before.

She hadn't even climbed the stairs to a bedroom but stayed where she was and wept out all the pain and regret she felt for what she had done to Will. She'd sobbed for the loss of her grandmother, for the loss of her own parents so many years ago and even for the errors in judgment she'd made while practicing law.

She should have told Will what she was considering from the beginning. He'd had a right to know. But she hadn't been sure herself. What good would it have done to get him stirred up unnecessarily? He was plenty stirred up now, though, and she had no idea how to rectify what she'd done.

How was she to know how much he abhorred a lack of honesty? And how was she to know how much she was going to care when he stormed out of her house and probably her life? All the justification in the world wouldn't change the fact that she hadn't been one-hundred-percent honest.

Stiffly, she rose from the couch and made her way upstairs to lie down again. While she turned back her covers she looked around the room. Will's touch was everywhere in the house now.

What a fool she'd been. She'd rolled in here like a misplaced general, giving orders and making decisions about things she knew little or nothing about. He'd deserved better. Abigail had trusted Will Tanner implicitly. He'd proved his worth by not holding a grudge against Catherine because she refused to represent him in court—and she still hadn't trusted him enough to talk to him about selling the house.

Catherine didn't know how to undo the mess she had on her hands now, but she could remedy a little of the damage she'd done. She'd take care of it as soon as she could.

As Catherine power walked down Main Street she saw Becky waving to her from the front door of her store, but she didn't cross the street to talk. She didn't want to visit with anyone right now. She was still too emotional to risk it.

She entered Travers & Travers law office and smiled weakly at the receptionist. "Hi, Wendy, how are you today?"

"Good. Are you looking for Jerry?" Catherine had known Wendy Burke since she was a little girl, and now she was all grown up. Continuity, that's what one got in a small town. No one she knew in the city ever seemed to stay in one place for long.

"I know it's early. Is he in yet?"

"He just got here. Go on in."

Catherine stuck her head around the corner of the door to Jerry's office. "Hello, anybody here?"

Jerry appeared from beneath his desk, an electrical cord in his hand. "Just us repair men. I kicked something and unplugged the power to everything on my desk. I'm glad I hadn't turned on my computer yet today." He slid into his chair. "What can I do for you?"

"I have a favor to ask of you."

"Shoot." Jerry leaned back in the chair to listen.

She told him about Will's situation with Charley and how she'd refused to take his case.

"Now he wouldn't let me represent him even if I begged him." For more reasons than one. "But he respects you. Would you offer to take his case? Will is the best parent Charley could have, Jerry. I want to do everything in my power to see that he keeps the child. What do you say?"

"I'm a general practitioner in a small town. Granted, I'm considered to be pretty good, but I don't have a backlog of experience with this sort of thing. How would you play into this?"

"I have the experience. If you represent Will, I'll come on as a consultant. I can tell you exactly how to play this thing out. I've done it enough times to be of help."

"I'm sure you have, Catherine, but I don't understand why you don't just do it yourself. You can work out of this office. I'll hire you right now."

"Will and I aren't on speaking terms. I did a very foolish thing. I kept some information from him that he deserved to know. He's very angry with me."

Curiosity was written across Jerry's face, but discreet man that he was, he didn't inquire further. The question he did ask, however, went like a dart to the center of its target. "If you are already in trouble with him for not being transparent, what would he think if he discovered you were in the background pulling the strings on this case?"

Catherine sat very still. *Lord, I just did it again, didn't I? Forgive me.*

"Perhaps that is one of the reasons I need to change careers, Jerry. It's too easy to leave the facts out that don't benefit my clients. I never thought of it as lying, but I suppose it is, in Will's eyes." *And God's.*

Do not lie to one another, seeing that you have stripped off the old self with its practices....

Obviously, she'd needed to return to Pleasant to get clear and to realize that the moral girl she'd been had shifted slightly off course.

"Tell Will I gave you his name. Tell him I'll be consulting but not actually representing him. And don't let him turn down your offer of help. You must make sure he agrees to work with you—in spite of me."

The attorney gave her a troubled look. However, when he spoke, all he said was, "I'm pleased to be working with you, Catherine, even under these conditions." Jerry thrust out his hand and Catherine took it.

Relief flooded through her. If nothing else, she

would do all she could to help Will keep Charley. He deserved that much.

Catherine took her time walking home, stopping at the drugstore to buy something for the headache she was developing. She bought a soda and swallowed the pills before she even left the store, strolling home slowly, hoping they would start to take effect.

When she neared Hope House, however, a headache of a different kind appeared on the horizon.

Regina Reynolds had returned. Catherine clenched her teeth. Did the woman have any sensibilities at all? She was as perceptive and aware of another's feelings as a clam. For someone who had never actually been given a go-ahead to sell the house, she was certainly busy doing so.

Catherine had a mind to tell Regina exactly what she thought of her, but there was another woman with her. Regina and the woman were standing in the front admiring the peonies.

"Catherine!" Regina sang out when she saw her approaching, "There's someone here I'd like you to meet." She took the woman by the hand and towed her in Catherine's direction. "This is Melanie Rose. She and her husband are the people I told you about, the ones in love with Hope House."

Catherine pasted a pained smile on her face and tried to remember her manners.

"We just love Hope House," the woman gushed. "It's absolutely perfect!"

Catherine could see why Melanie would be a good hostess for a B and B. She had overwhelming enthusiasm for everything. Catherine couldn't think of a way to respond. The whole mess had left her speechless.

"If we make it into a B and B we'd have to change the name, of course," Melanie chattered. "Hope House is lovely and all, but we own several B and B's with similar names. I'm thinking this one could be Rose House. That wouldn't be such a change, would it? We'd make up a brochure telling the house's history, of course. We wouldn't want that to be forgotten. I'm so glad you got here, Catherine. Regina said she was sure you would show us around."

Melanie continued, "I'll get my husband. He's out back with your gardener."

Gardener? Catherine's heart sank. "I'll get them. You keep looking around. I'll be right back." She escaped before either woman had a chance to stop her.

How was she going to get out of this? Everything was out of control. If Will had been angry before, he'd be apoplectic now.

She came upon the two men quietly. They were staring at the house's foundation and carrying on a laconic conversation.

"Foundation needs work," she heard Will say. "I've got a start on replacing the grout on the inside, but now that I look at it, I see that there will have to be some repairs out here, as well. I can give you the name of a man I know who moves houses. Maybe he can tell you what you'll need to do. You may have to lift it off its foundation to do it right, of course."

What was Will doing?

"He can tell you, too, if you'll need to rebuild the porches. I've been meaning to get under them to see how badly they've deteriorated. Good thing I fixed up the main bathroom. You'll have that one operational while you redo the others…."

"You think we'll have to do that?" Mr. Rose inquired, sounding worried.

"That's up to you. Your guests will notice, of course. No expense was spared on the renovations, but I figure you could do each bathroom for…"

He threw out a number that made Catherine wince.

"That's what the previous owner planned to spend on them," Will said amiably.

Mr. Rose paled.

Catherine had had no idea the extent of the financial commitment Gram had made to this project.

"That much?" Mr. Rose's voice was a little unsteady. "That's what I usually plan for an entire house renovation."

Will looked at him benevolently. "But this is Hope House. You can't cut corners on what will be the jewel of your B and B's."

"I suppose that's true...."

Will was talking Mr. Rose out of buying the house just as quickly as Regina was trying to talk Mrs. Rose into it! Catherine supposed she should have been upset with him, but instead it struck her as funny.

Regina Reynolds had met her match in Will Tanner. And Will hadn't said anything that wasn't true. He just didn't point out how much of the house was magnificent. Rather, he'd helped Mr. Rose focus on the flaws. If selling a home was a spectator sport, Will would be Regina's toughest competitor.

Catherine found herself cheering for Will.

Mr. Rose took a small notebook out of his shirt pocket and made some notes.

Catherine cleared her throat.

Will spun around, caught in the act. He appeared unrepentant. "Catherine!"

Before she could introduce herself to the concerned-looking Mr. Rose, Regina and Melanie rounded the corner of the house.

"Oh, sweetheart, isn't this magnificent? I can hardly wait to look inside...." Regina bobbed her head in agreement.

"Honey, I think you and I should have a conversation about this before we get *too* excited."

Regina and Melanie stared at him, mouths open. "Why? It's perfect!"

"It is lovely, there's no doubt about that. But I've been talking to Mr. Tanner about a few things, the foundation, for one, the safety and sturdiness of the porches and the guest bathrooms…."

"We can take care of all that," Melanie said with a wave of her hand. "We've done it several times."

"Mr. Tanner gave me the cost estimates that he got for the late Mrs. Stanhope. They're…significant." He held out the little notebook to his wife.

Melanie glanced at the scribbles and her eyes widened. "That much?"

"At least," Will added unhelpfully. "Too bad you didn't wait to come around after the place was finished. It was going to be a beauty." His eyes widened and a look of sheer innocence came over him. "Are there any other questions I can answer for you?"

Regina, her expression frantic, stepped forward. "I think you've helped enough, Mr. Tanner." She turned to Catherine. "Don't you?"

She had no idea what came over her, but Catherine burst out laughing. "It seems to me that Mr. Tanner has been very ready to lend a hand." Strangely, she felt only relief. Maybe she wasn't so eager to sell Hope House after all. Besides, Rose House sounded like the name of someone's greenhouse, not a place as wonderful as this.

Marveling at her unexpected about-face, she moved to stand by Will—a show of support, perhaps?

Chapter Nineteen

Will and Catherine watched Mr. and Mrs. Rose hurry down the driveway to their car. Regina trotted behind them assuring them in a loud voice that if they would only look inside the house, they would see that the foundation and the bathrooms were passable.

Finally Catherine turned to Will. "Well, you sabotaged that rather nicely."

"I didn't tell anything but the truth. You saw the plan Abigail and I drew up for restoring the house."

"And at such an opportune time, too." She marveled that she didn't mind. She almost felt like a coconspirator.

"You wouldn't want to sell a place without revealing everything to the potential buyers. That's not ethical."

"It appears that Regina isn't quite as ethical as you."

Will forehead creased in a frown. "Obviously. How did you get hooked up with her anyway? Around Pleasant she's known as pushy and overbearing."

Catherine started toward the porch and Will followed. "I didn't 'hook up' with her. She just appeared and started to try to sell the place."

"You didn't approach her first?"

"No. Like I said before, I seriously considered selling Hope House. I saw no way to live in it and still pursue the life I'd planned. In fact, I thought I'd decided to do it, but once I was here for a while, I realized that too much was going on and that I wasn't sure of my own mind."

"The life you'd planned?"

"Teaching law for a while. Then who knows what," Catherine said absently. "Regina approached me. I met her when she came into Becky's Attic to make some purchases. You were there when she appeared on my doorstep to tell me she found buyers without even having my permission to look for purchasers. She also brought them here today unannounced. Ms. Reynolds assumes a lot."

"You aren't going to sell Hope House?"

"I didn't say that." Catherine chewed at her lower lip. "All I know is that when I recognized that there was someone ready to put their money down, it wasn't as easy as I thought it would be."

"Then you aren't mad at me?" Will looked like

Charley after he'd dropped a bowl of oatmeal on the kitchen floor. Charley was sorry the bowl had broken, but sorrier still that he'd missed his breakfast. It was too late, of course, now that Will had chased Regina and the Roses away. At least he had the good sense to be contrite.

"Actually, I'm furious with you. If I hadn't already been second-guessing myself and had wanted to sell the house immediately, you would have ruined everything."

He looked a little too happy about it all, but she couldn't muster up the energy to be upset with him. "We're probably even now. Besides being aggravated with you, I'm a little grateful. This clarified for me that I'm not ready to make that decision quite yet." She eyed him appraisingly. "You skirted my wrath by this much." She held her thumb and forefinger a hairbreadth apart.

"The question is, then—" his eyes narrowed as he studied her "—what do we do next?"

She wasn't as angry with him as he'd feared. Nor was she walking away from Hope House or from him—at least not yet. Will was amazed by the relief he felt. Until this moment he hadn't known exactly how much his relationship with her meant to him. *Everything. It meant everything.*

"Is there anything I can do to make it up to you?" He'd botched up so much that she probably didn't want him touching anything, but he felt he had to make the offer anyway.

"Yes, there is." Her chin came up in that feisty way of hers and he felt like putting his forefinger beneath her jaw and tilting her head a bit more so he'd have easy access to her lips.

Suspicion reared its ugly head. "I need to hear what it is first," Will said cautiously.

"Promise me you'll do it?"

"No way, lady. We've had enough trouble already with a lack of communication."

"I suppose you're right," she said with a sigh. She looked at him coyly, tilting her chin toward him. A tiny smiled played on her lips.

Will felt suddenly giddy. Maybe he still had a chance with her. A chance at what, he wasn't sure— friendship, romance, civility—but whatever it was, he'd take it.

"I want you to go to Jerry Travers and hire him to be your attorney. He's already agreed to represent you. I asked him."

He didn't know what to say. What was she up to now?

"You did, did you? Why Jerry? There are lots of attorneys around."

"Because, although I won't represent you, I will consult with Jerry. I can help him by sharing my experience. There's no reason that you shouldn't get custody of Charley with the two of us on your team."

"You'd do that? I thought…" He was surprised and touched.

"I know what I said. But I can't let Charley suffer. I need to do what I can to help him. Besides, I won't be the one officially representing you. I'll be behind the scenes. I'm more comfortable with that."

Will felt an unfamiliar thickening in his throat. If he wasn't careful, the next thing he might do was tear up. "Catherine, I…"

"Don't say it. Let's just get busy. I just came from Travers & Travers. We can catch him there if we go now." She caught him by the hand and pulled him in the direction of Main Street.

As they walked together toward Jerry's office, Will desperately wanted to put his arm around her to catch the scent of her perfume and feel her warmth. They'd just skirted a clash of wills, however, and he wasn't fool enough to do that quite yet. It might feel as though he had the tiger by the tail right now, but he knew this little tiger could scratch.

When they got to the office, Wendy waved them in, as if Jerry were expecting them. With a few quick words and a handshake the deal was set. Travers & Travers and Stanhope were now on his team. *Team Charley.*

Will was impressed in spite of himself when he

saw Catherine spin into action. She and Jerry talked a mile a minute as Will listened. They used yellow legal pads to take notes and chatted in a form of legalese that Will didn't speak.

With one ear still attuned to the conversation, he drifted into his own train of thought. He contemplated his brother, Matt. There was something very wrong with Matt's relationship with Sheila, but Will still couldn't put a finger on it. Sheila was difficult, sure, and domineering. Matt had always been fairly passive but still capable of fending for himself. That had changed in the past five or six years. And ever since Annie had died, he'd acted even odder.

His brother had not always been the doormat he was now, not by a long shot. It had begun to change when he started dating Sheila and had snowballed even more since Annie's death.

As Catherine had suggested, Sheila had to have something over on him to make Matt acquiesce to her demands. She couldn't be protecting him. There was nothing to be protected from.

"Don't you think that's a prudent plan, Will?" Jerry Travers's voice broke into Will's reverie.

He jerked as he sat up straight. "Sorry, I wasn't listening. What did you say?"

"What is more important than this case?" Catherine wanted to know. Her eyes narrowed. "Have you thought of something?"

"I'm not sure it's relevant. Maybe it's just how my brother is now," his voice trailed away for a moment. "You mentioned it once, Catherine. There has to be a reason that Matt is allowing Sheila to go ahead with this. I doubt very much he'd challenge me if it weren't for his wife. If I knew what my brother was thinking, it might make a difference. At least then we could talk man-to-man without having Sheila as his go-between. There's something funny about the way Matt has allowed Sheila to lead the charge."

"You've already tried to talk to him?"

"A dozen times. Sheila is pasted to him like wallpaper. She doesn't allow the two of us to talk privately. I suppose she assumes I'll undermine her with Matt."

"Would you?" Jerry inquired.

"I might have at one time, but I'm a different man now. Thank God." Will meant that with all his heart.

"We'll move ahead anyway," Jerry said, "but it might benefit you if you could discover what your brother is thinking. Maybe he's not so gung ho about this adoption as his wife is. On the other hand, he may be the one who's really propelling the action."

Maybe, but Will doubted it.

"When are you going to talk to Matt?" Catherine asked after they'd left Jerry's office. It felt wonderful to be working together. Things were different now that they'd both allowed their initial attraction to blossom.

"No time like the present." Will pulled his cell phone out of his pocket, found his brother's name in the address book and hit Send.

"Matt here."

Will held the phone slightly away from his ear so that Catherine could hear. "Matt, it's Will. Listen, buddy, what are you doing right now?"

"It's funny that you called. I'm not too far from Pleasant on a sales call. Why?"

"I'd like to get together. Could you swing by here?"

The hesitance in Matt's voice was apparent. "I don't know...."

"Come on, bro. When's the last time we really talked?" Will cajoled.

"Maybe Sheila and I could run up there..."

"You're in the neighborhood and you want to drive home, get your wife and come back?" Disbelief was heavy in Will's voice. "You're kidding, right?"

Matt gave in reluctantly. "I could be there in an hour, maybe, after I'm done with my client."

"Deal. Come by Hope House. Just ring the doorbell when you get here." Before Matt could protest or find his way out, Will hung up.

"Now we'll have to wait and see if he actually shows up."

Back at Hope House, she and Will sat across from each other waiting. Time, which was often so fleeting, dragged on like an eternity when she was waiting for something to happen. It was just as difficult for Will. That was obvious by the look of misery on his handsome features.

He was the one, of course, who had the right to be nervous. It was he who had to convince his brother that it was confession time if, as they expected, there was something to confess. Or maybe Matt and Sheila were simply difficult people who wanted to punish Will at Charley's expense, Catherine thought, although she could not imagine it.

When the doorbell rang, they both reacted as if they'd been shot, and jumped to their feet in unison. Before they got to the door, Will put his hand on Catherine's arm. "No matter what my brother says, I want you to stay in the room."

"It may get very personal," she reminded him.

"I don't care. All I want to do is to understand why he is behaving this way. And I want you to hear it, too."

She expelled a breath of air. "Okay, but it might not be pretty."

"Pretty doesn't matter anymore."

When Will opened the door, Matt was standing on the other side with his hands in his pockets, his shoulders hunched.

"Come on in, Matt." Will stepped aside so his brother could enter. "Welcome."

Matt's eyes were on Catherine. "Wha—"

"She owns the house and I invited her to stay. I didn't think you'd mind, considering you always have Sheila along when you talk to me."

Matt didn't seem to know how to respond. Catherine quietly faded into the background, willing herself to disappear into the furnishings, hoping he'd forget she was there.

"I don't know what there is to talk about, Will." Matt jumped right into the topic at hand. "The wheels to get custody of Charley have been set in motion. You're a single guy living in somebody's guesthouse, for goodness' sake. What's that compared to a child having two parents and a real home? I wish you'd just quit fighting Sheila on this." Matt looked miserable and uncomfortable.

"So it's Sheila I'm fighting? Not the two of you?"

Matt looked stricken. "Of course it's both of us. I just meant…"

Will ushered him into the living room and into the stiffest, most uncomfortable horsehair couch in the room.

Catherine took a chair in a dim corner and continued to make herself inconspicuous.

"What do you mean? I've been wondering for years, Matt. I remember the days when you and I were best friends. When you came to me for advice." Will chuckled without humor. "Of course, I did give you some advice about Sheila that you didn't take."

Matt winced. "She was very upset, Will. She thought she was going to lose me because of you."

"Because I expressed my opinion I was forced to give up a relationship with you entirely? Come on, Matt, where's your spine? You know that I'd give Sheila every chance despite my original impressions. I'm not a troublemaker." Will sounded disgusted now, his features settling into a scowl. "You do know that, right? Or have you forgotten?"

"I haven't forgotten anything," Matt blurted. "It's just a lot more complicated than you realize. I can't... Sheila will... Just stay out of it, okay? Stay out of my life. You'll be better off."

"No way. If Sheila thinks getting Charley will get rid of me, she's wrong. I'm going to be camped on your doorstep every weekend. I'll be in her face every holiday. Why, the two of you will see more of me in a month than you have in the last three years."

Matt looked at his brother askance. "You're just saying that."

"I mean it with every fiber in my being. Annie asked me to raise Charley and I gave her my word. I plan to keep it."

Matt's whole body seemed to slump at the sound of his sister's name.

Catherine, accustomed to watching and listening for visual and verbal cues and taking the emotional temperature of anyone she had on the witness stand, jumped into the conversation.

"What's Sheila holding over you, Matt?" She kept her voice soothing, comforting. No use backing him into a corner and forcing him to fight his way out. "There's got to be something that has kept you estranged from your brother all these years. It's going to come out. Secrets always do." She knew that from personal experience.

It was no wonder Will had no tolerance for furtiveness if this was his life experience.

She watched Matt and recognized the posture of someone on the witness stand about to say something that he'd never planned to admit, something that had weighed upon him so long that he simply couldn't hold back any longer.

"My wife and I are both messed up, Will, but for different reasons. Sheila is so desperate for a child that it's driven her half-crazy. The doctors have told her she's infertile and she can't accept it. She thinks

Charley is her only way to be a mother. I've told her we can adopt. Lots of kids, if she wants, but it's as if she doesn't hear me."

"But that doesn't explain why she's got such an iron grip on you, Matt." Will's tone had softened and there was real compassion for Matt in his eyes.

"Sheila knows something that I never wanted you or anyone else to find out." As Matt looked at Will his lips turned down at the corners. "I thought you'd strangle me with your bare hands if you knew, so I made her promise never to say a thing."

He worked his fingers through his finely groomed hair until it stood on end. "What I didn't expect to happen was that she'd use it to get her own way.

"Sheila can carry a grudge, Will, and she's always wanted to punish you for trying to save me from her." Matt looked utterly miserable. Then he rallied a bit. "She's not difficult all the time, you know. She can be very sweet and thoughtful."

Will leaned forward, attempting to capture Matt's gaze with his own. "What's this awful thing, Matt? Wouldn't it be better to get it out? It's pretty much ruined our relationship anyway. It's given your wife the power to manipulate you."

"I've regretted it for years, Will, but there's no way to go back and repair the damage." Matt's clenched and unclenched his fists and tears welled in his eyes.

Catherine realized she was holding her breath.

"I'm responsible for Annie's death. If it hadn't been for me, she might still be alive. She might never have started drinking." Matt dropped his head into his hands. "I killed her, Will, one drink at a time."

Chapter Twenty

"That's what you've been carrying around all these years?" Will asked.

"I realize now how vulnerable Annie was when she was young, but at the time I had no idea. I wasn't that much older than her and..."

"What are you saying?" Will's insides tightened.

Matt finally lifted his head to look Will in the eye. "I'm the person who gave Annie her first drink. And her second."

Will forced himself to sit silently while his brother rambled through his weighty confession.

"She was fourteen and I was seventeen."

"She was practically a baby."

"You'd already left home. I took her to some parties with me, that was all. I thought we could have some fun."

"What kind of fun is that, Matt?"

"Annie really missed you after you left home and

I wanted to show her a good time. Mom and Dad depended on me to take care of her, so they let her go."

Matt looked as if he was about to cry. "I've broken every trust I've been given.

"We were underage and it was stupid and dangerous. Like every other teenager I knew, I thought I was invincible—and so did Annie."

"But how…"

"After a while I lost interest in hard partying, but Annie…"

Will felt a lump in his throat. "Kept on drinking when the parties stopped?" He didn't recognize his own voice when he spoke.

"We did some drugs together, too," Matt choked out. "Not much. She didn't go for that, not like alcohol."

Will groaned and scraped his fingers through his hair.

"I caught her drinking alone in her room several times," Matt said. "I don't know where she got the stuff and she wouldn't tell me. I assumed she'd lose interest after a while, like with the drugs, but it wasn't long before I realized she had a problem, a big one."

"And then what did you do?"

"Nothing. She didn't think it was an issue. She *liked* what she was doing. When she couldn't find someone to buy her what she wanted. she'd beg me to do it. *Beg* me. She'd say, 'You're the one who introduced me to this, Matt, you can't abandon me now.'"

Will felt his blood rising. "So you kept on getting it for her?"

"I can't believe I did. I knew that Annie could find others to buy the stuff for her, but I still did it. Her own brother. I should have been punching some guy's lights out for mistreating my sister. Instead I was the one mistreating her!"

"Matt, I don't know what to say."

"She'd be sober for long stretches, Will." There was a pleading tone in Matt's voice. "It wasn't like daily or weekly—even monthly—but you know how Annie could be. She could talk wallpaper off a wall and sell ice to Eskimos. I felt guilty but I didn't turn her down. I was immature enough to think she'd get over it."

Will had never seen such self-loathing in his brother's eyes.

"I was an enabler. I see that now. I'm not like you, Will. You're independent and strong. You live by a set of admirable values. You're a Christian and I'm a weak, stupid man who's messed up not only his own life but that of his sister. What's more, my wife's a desperately unhappy woman who wants to put a knife in your back. Get away from us—for your own sake."

"It doesn't have to be this way..." Will began, but Matt stopped him.

"You have no idea how I suffered when our sister was diagnosed with cirrhosis. I wanted to die if only I could save Annie. I was the one responsible for making her an alcoholic."

"You can't take all that on yourself," Will said, his voice controlled. "Annie made her own decisions. I can't tell you how many times I tried to get her into treatment and she refused or checked herself out. She would have found what she wanted without you."

"It doesn't matter. I betrayed her. I let her down. I should have been taking care of her when all I was doing was looking out for myself." Matt tugged at his tie. "I'm so weak and pathetic I can't even look myself in the mirror."

"And Sheila?" Will asked. He was monitoring his emotions carefully. He didn't want to do or say anything he would regret later.

With a groan, Matt put his head into his hands. "That's a whole different story."

"Then you'd better tell me that one, too."

"I told Sheila how I'd enabled Annie. I was crazy in love with Sheila and thought that I'd show her how much I trusted her by telling her my deep, dark secret. She took it all in and didn't say anything about it for a long time, but when she got wind of what you thought of her, she started using it against me."

Will struggled to take in this complicated mental and emotional trail his brother had taken.

"Every time she wanted her way—like uninviting you to a family gathering—she said that if I didn't go along with her she would tell you everything she knew about Annie and me." Matt's features contorted and he took a deep, ragged breath. "In some weird way I think Sheila actually thought she might be protecting me from you."

Will didn't know if he was disgusted, repulsed or just plain sad about this turn of events.

"I've made a mess of everyone's lives," Matt said matter-of-factly. "It's time I took full responsibility for that."

"I wish you'd decided that sooner," Will said. "If I'd known, I would never have let our relationship falter like it did."

Matt's eyes widened. "Really?"

"If you'd told me these things years ago, yeah, I would have been furious with you," Will admitted. "Punched you out, maybe, but I wouldn't have disowned you. Everybody makes mistakes."

He'd come a long way, Will realized. He was upset with Matt—first for being a stupid teenager and second for not trusting him with his concerns—but he wasn't as angry as he'd expected he might be. He was saddened, yes, but resentful or vengeful, no. He'd been forgiven after all. What else could he do but forgive Matt?

"So you mean…" Matt allowed the question to trail away. For the first time in a long while, he looked directly into his brother's eyes.

"I'm still your brother and I love you," Will said simply. "Annie died knowing she was going to heaven. She also knew I'd promised to raise Charley. It was probably as good an ending as she could get for her short, ill-fated life. I forgive you and I know Annie would, too."

Tears began to roll down Matt's cheeks as Will spoke.

"This problem is about you and Sheila. It's not about you and me. You've allowed her to manipulate you so long that you've grown accustomed to it and you've made excuses for her behavior because she can't have a child. What I hear you saying is that Sheila isn't a bad person but a totally misguided one."

Will leaned forward, intent on making Matt truly hear what he had to say. "You see why I can't let you and Sheila have Charley, don't you? It's for your sakes as well as his. It's going to take time and work to smooth things out in your marriage. Adopting Charley as a way to hurt me could destroy everything for all of us."

* * *

Catherine moved quietly to stand beside Will, her hand on his shoulder. "We'll make sure you have generous visiting rights. You can come here anytime you want. Charley can also visit you. It's important, however, that Charley feel secure. I have a hunch it's not going to feel very stable at your house for a while."

"You think?" Matt smiled wanly, the color returning to his face. "Do you know what the crazy thing is?" Matt murmured. "I still love her. After all this, I still love her."

"Sheila's a lucky woman. The two of you will work it out."

Matt rose to his feet. "You're right, of course. We have no business bringing a child into this mess. Besides, I can't think of a man who would be a better influence on Charley than Will."

Will stood and the brothers embraced. Catherine felt something loosen within her. Charley would be fine now. They all would be. Except, perhaps, Sheila.

"I'm going home to talk to Sheila right now," Matt said, almost as if he'd read Catherine's mind. "If you hear any nuclear explosions coming from that direction, just ignore them. It will be Sheila spouting off." He shook his head. "She's going to be upset."

"She can deal with it," Catherine said.

"You're right. She can. It's time I behaved like a husband instead of a lump of clay. We have a lot to work through."

"Good luck." Will put his arm around his brother's shoulders. "I'll be praying for you."

Catherine tucked her hand through the crook of Will's arm. "*We'll* be praying for you."

When Matt had left, Will turned to Catherine. She tipped her head to look up at him and smiled. "Well done, Will."

"An answer to prayer." He studied her so intently that she was tempted to look away.

"So this means we're friends now?" he asked.

"We've always been friends, Will. From the day I met you I knew you were a good man."

"You did? Why did you keep me at arm's length so long?"

"Gram knew who to trust. I should have been as smart as she from day one."

Catherine felt a blush coming on. "I apologize to you for not telling you my thoughts from the beginning, about the house and everything else."

"You didn't know back then how much I hate secrets."

"All I knew when I arrived here was that I wasn't happy with my life. I wanted to move on. I'd committed to teach some law classes and thought I needed to sell the house. Now it just doesn't seem very urgent anymore."

Catherine pulled away. "I have something I'd like to give you."

"Me? Why?"

"Just wait, you'll see." She went into the dining room where she'd hidden the package Ellen had sent her and took it to him.

"Open it."

"I don't have anything for you."

"That doesn't matter. Gifts aren't always meant to be reciprocated."

He undid the brown paper to reveal two thick pieces of flat cardboard. He held them up to the light. "Lovely," he teased. "Just what I've always wanted."

"Look inside."

Will lifted one piece of cardboard and set it aside. There, in front of them, was a photo of Charley smiling out at them. Ellen had captured his personality completely. The sensitivity, the joy, the curiosity, the love, they were all there in those shining eyes and happy smile. Will stared at it, dumbfounded.

"Where…when…"

"My aunt Ellen was in the area. Charley and I wanted to surprise you. Do you like it?"

"Like it? It is absolutely amazing, the best gift I've ever received…." He touched the photo and it slid aside to reveal a second picture beneath. "What's this?"

"I don't know. The top picture is the one I ordered from my aunt."

He moved the picture away to reveal one of Catherine and Charley sitting together studying a caterpillar on Charley's finger. Charley was resting against Catherine, as though curling against her was the most comfortable and natural thing in the world. She was leaning forward, her golden hair half obscuring her face. The two of them appeared lost in a wonderful world of their own.

"She must have put that one in because she liked it," Catherine said. "Otherwise I don't know how it got there."

"I'm glad she did. It only affirms what I have to say to you."

"What's that?"

"Just like Abigail and I had a dream for the house, I have one for you." He tucked her beneath his arm.

They walked outside to the porch swing and rocked the swing silently for a few moments.

"About that dream…" she began.

"Oh, yes." He smiled at her. "My dream is that you stay in Pleasant for a very long time. That you work with Becky or Jerry or whoever else you want. Teach and plan to commute, if you have to. It's not like the nearest law school is in Timbuktu. For a year or two at least."

"Only a year or two?"

"Yes, because by that time, Charley and I will have moved into Hope House with you and you'll be expecting Charley's little brother or sister. You won't have time to work much outside the home after that. Especially not with another baby on the way only two years after the first." He looked at her with so much love in his eyes that it nearly took her breath away.

"Two babies?"

"At least. Maybe four. You were an only child. You really should know what it is like to have a big family."

"I should, should I?"

"Definitely. It's part of my dream for you."

"There's more?"

"Yes, but I might be getting ahead of myself. There's kindergarten to deal with, grade school, teenagers, sending them all to college…and grandchildren someday. Frankly, I think Hope House deserves a chance at being a family home again, don't you?"

"Are you suggesting this all for the sake of Hope House?"

"Not one hundred percent, of course…."

"Let me get one thing straight. Was there a marriage proposal in there somewhere, or wasn't that part of your dream?"

"Catherine," Will said, "that is my dream. Will you marry me?"

She tapped her chin with one finely shaped fingernail and smiled at him. "Let me see…you're offering me a husband, a child, a handyman, a home filled with children and a chance to grow old with you, is that right?"

"The handyman will work for free, by the way. Perhaps that'll sweeten the deal."

"In that case, I accept. It's so hard to find good help these days."

"Darling, I've just signed a contract for life."

Epilogue

Becky was playing the harp and Little Eddie was serving appetizers by the time Will and Catherine had completed shaking hands in the receiving line. Charley, Will's best man, and Matt, his groomsman, were already outside tying the dozens of tin cans Emma had collected onto Will's vehicle.

Sheila was sitting in the far corner of the room with Regina Reynolds. The two women looked as if they were in a dentist's waiting room, but at least they were present.

Whatever had transpired between Matt and his wife, neither Will nor Catherine knew, but the custody suit had disappeared without being pursued.

Catherine and Will headed directly for the two women.

"Congratulations, Catherine, Will. I suppose you won't be selling the house now," Regina said. She had the grace to blush.

"We'll be living in it for a long time ourselves, God willing."

Will turned to Sheila. "I'm glad you're here. It wouldn't have been right to have this wedding without you."

Her features were sharp and pale and the misery in her expression was real.

"Will, I need to apologize…."

He put his hand on her arm. "We can talk later, Sheila. Right now I want you to know I've missed having you and Matt in my life. Today is a day of new beginnings for Catherine and me and, hopefully, for you and Matt—and the relationship between us as couples. Our home is open to you. All three of us will be glad to see you anytime."

Sheila stared at them intently, as if she couldn't believe what she was hearing.

"Forgiveness is to be passed on, not hoarded. The more you give, the more you have."

"I'll remember that."

Will leaned over and hugged her.

What was even more wonderful, Catherine observed, was that Sheila hugged him back.

Lilly, Catherine's friend from the city, floated their way. "I can't believe how wonderful a place this is, Catherine. Why didn't you tell me?"

"I tried. You said it was nowheresville, if I remember correctly." Catherine recalled Lilly's raptures about the beauty of Hope House, the sweetness of Charley and the handsome deliciousness of Will.

"I was *so* wrong." Lilly's eyes narrowed. "The caterer, Eddie? Do you think he's married?"

"Don't tell me, Lilly, you'd leave it all to come to the country?" Catherine teased.

"Eddie is single," Will said succinctly. "And looking."

"Bliss," Lilly murmured and wandered off in the direction of the kitchen.

"You don't think Eddie would…" Catherine began.

"Once he sees how happy I am, he just might." Will steered her behind a decorative tree strung with white lights and wedding bells to steal a kiss.

Catherine thrust her left hand upward, into his face. "Maybe you'd like to explain this?"

Abigail Stanhope's wedding ring fit neatly onto Catherine's finger. He'd surprised her with it at the altar and brought on a flood of happy tears that had threatened to wash the wedding party away.

"I'm not quite sure how, Catherine. A few months back, Abigail told me where she kept it. She said that she wanted me to know where it was, so if anything happened to her, I would be able to give it to you. She didn't want it overlooked."

"Why didn't you give it to me the day I arrived?"

Will flushed beneath his white starched collar.

"I'd planned to. But there was something about you…and something Abigail had said."

Catherine, hearing all this for the first time, was confused. "What was that?"

His face grew even redder. "She said that she'd like me for a grandson-in-law."

Catherine's jaw dropped.

"She also said that if you had the sense you were born with, you'd make sure that happened." He ran his fingers through his hair. "She kind of gave me permission to marry you, Catherine. So I kept the ring from you for a few weeks just to, well, you know."

"See if I worked out?" Catherine's grin grew wider by the moment. "So you *do* keep secrets, Will Tanner."

"That's the last one, I promise."

The traditional clatter of spoons on glasses in the reception hall signaled that the guests wanted to see a kiss from the bride and groom.

"Shall we give them what they want?" Will asked.

Catherine put her hand in his and led the way. "It seems only right to share our happiness."

* * * * *

Dear Reader,

Are you sentimental? Do you have a difficult time parting with things that hold memories of your childhood, family members or loved ones? Or are you content with having just the memories and happy to give up the "stuff" itself? I have one daughter who is exceedingly sentimental. I once found a chocolate Easter bunny in her closet that had turned white with age because she felt it was too precious to eat. Who knows how long she'd kept it hidden! I also have a daughter who falls more on the side of "if you haven't used it in a year, throw it out."

In *Mending Her Heart,* Catherine Stanhope has both problems. A city girl, she can't imagine living in her family's mansion in the tiny town of Pleasant, Minnesota. Surprisingly, however, when she decides to give up the mansion, it's more of a struggle than she'd imagined. All this is exacerbated by the handsome handyman she inherited right along with the house. He doesn't want her to sell her grandmother's home—for some very personal reasons of his own.

I hope you'll enjoy the story that shows how repairing a house can lead to something unexpected—the mending of one's heart. I'd love to hear from you. Feel free to write to me in care of Steeple Hill, 233 Broadway, Suite 1001, New York, New York, 10279.

Sincerely,

Judy

QUESTIONS FOR DISCUSSION

1. One of the reasons Catherine Stanhope decided to quit her job was that she felt she'd made a mistake (although unintentional) that hurt someone. Have you ever felt like walking away from a job, organization or group because you felt guilty about something? Looking back, was it the right thing to do? Do you regret your decision or are you glad you made it?

2. If you inherited a beautiful home in a place that you didn't want to live, what would you do? Sell it? Try to live there anyway? What do you think might happen if you chose to live in a house you loved in a location you didn't like?

3. Have you been given an antique or memento by a loved one that you really didn't want or need? What did you do with it?

4. Will wants to make a home for his nephew, Charley, but his married brother and sister-in-law think they should adopt him because there are two of them and they would make a "real" family. How do you respond to this?

5. Who was your favorite character—Catherine, Will, Charley or someone else? Did you relate personally to any of them? Did any of them remind you of someone you know? How?

6. Catherine works in Becky's Attic, her friend's antiques shop, because she finds it interesting and tranquil. If you could choose a part-time job that you believe would be perfect for you, what would it be?

7. Have you run into pushy salespeople like the real-estate agent Regina Reynolds? How did you handle them?

8. Eddie's is a little restaurant in the middle of nowhere but it is a culinary treasure. Have you ever found any serendipitous places to dine that are in unexpected locations?

9. What did you think of Will's sister, Annie? Although she is gone before the book begins, she still has a good deal of influence on her brother and son. How have the decisions of other family members affected you? Has it been good or bad?

10. Matt Tanner sometimes appears to be a cowardly man. He's living a life besieged

by guilt. What do Christians know about carrying guilt and how to be free of it in their lives?

11. If you had a house the size of Hope House and could turn it into anything you wanted—a business like a restaurant or a store, headquarters for a charity or a school—what would you do? Why?

12. Catherine's grandmother, Abigail, is obviously a lovable meddler and she even manages to intervene from the grave. How would you respond to something like that? Would you welcome or resent it?

LARGER-PRINT BOOKS!

GET 2 FREE
LARGER-PRINT NOVELS
PLUS 2 FREE
MYSTERY GIFTS

Love Inspired®

Larger-print novels are now available...